THE RICH GUY'S WIFE

A TWISTY DOMESTIC THRILLER

BONNIE TRAYMORE

ALSO BY BONNIE TRAYMORE

Killer Motives

Little Loose Ends

The Stepfamily

The Guest House

Head Case

The Bluff

A Little Getaway

The Unforgetting

Swipe

*For Annie,
my wing woman*

PROLOGUE
ERIN

Mother's voice rings in my ears as I stand perfectly still in the darkness, fearing that each breath I take will be my last:

Be careful what you wish for, Erin.

I'm crouched down in the closet, my legs and back aching to move, even an inch. But I can't. One twitch, one cramp, and I'll bang into a shelf and give myself away.

Sweat beads form at my hairline, nagging at me as they threaten to drip down my face. I slide a hand up my side, being careful not to bang into anything, and wipe away the dampness. Perspiration mixes with the blood on my hand, reminding me of the carnage outside the door.

Why did I touch the body?

I always thought my mother said things like that to darken my dreams. To stave off the inevitable disappointment that comes from shooting too high in life and falling short. For daring to reach for the stars, only to have them slip through your fingers and fall away like glitter from a magic wand.

Nothing she said deterred me, though. Because I figured

something out pretty early on in life. In New York City, if you're not filthy rich, you're poor—and I was not going to end up like her.

But I see now that my mother spoke from experience.

She knew them.

Studied them.

Understood them.

The rich guys, and their wives.

What she really meant was:

Be careful what you're wishing for, Erin.

Because I got what I wished for.

I'm a rich guy's wife now.

And it just might be the death of me.

THE COURTSHIP
FOUR MONTHS EARLIER

ONE

ERIN

It's one of those magical Friday nights in Manhattan, full of hope and possibilities. It's nearly seven in the evening, and we're on the brink of summer, but a slight nip in the air remains. Soon, the summer swelter will arrive, dividing the haves and the have-nots, turning the city into a ghost town as far as the who's who and filling it with twenty-year-old college interns, out-of-town tourists, and bridge and tunnel weekend warriors. In short, time is running out.

I enter the bar guardedly optimistic, which is pretty much my go-to state. At heart, I'm an optimist, but that's been tempered over the years by my upbringing and life experiences. Still, a little uptick in my pulse tells me that hope lives in me, and as I search the crowd for my friend Lucy, I can't help but notice that the ratio is in our favor this evening.

Bumping up against a pack of twenty-something giggly girls, already tipsy but young enough to come off looking cute rather than pathetic, my biological clock ticks like a time bomb. I've been at this for far too long. At some point, I'll have to settle. Or move. Or something. At thirty-one, I still have some time, but not much.

"Hey, Erin," Lucy calls out, her hand shooting up from her perch at the bar.

We're aiming for the after-work crowd tonight. Lucy Chang is a star defense attorney, the kind who doesn't need a man to live large. We met in private school, lost touch, and then reconnected. Her dark, silky hair shimmers in the wash of the overhead lights. She's dressed in a gray pencil skirt and a soft white blouse, unbuttoned just enough to add a hint of sexy to her toughness.

I'm wearing a cobalt blue dress that hugs my body and brings out my eyes. Not too short, just above the knee, but with little slits on the sides that hint at what's underneath. We make good barfly partners, the two of us. The tall, thin brunette and the busty blonde.

"What'll you have?" she asks, snapping her fingers at the bartender.

The bartender glares at Lucy as he positions himself in front of me. He's cute. Really cute. But he's not the kind of guy I'm looking for. Still, he's a human being, and Lucy can be a little harsh sometimes. Plus, I don't want him to poison us.

"Sorry about my friend," I say to him with a smile. "She spends her days with hardened criminals."

"Guilty." Lucy offers an apologetic shrug.

He smiles back at me. "What can I get you?" he asks me.

"A champagne cocktail," I reply.

Lucy's saved me a seat, but it's three-deep at the bar and standing room only now. It's a large bar in a trendy restaurant. Koho, it's called. Just east of Grand Central, so we'll get the Westchester commuter crowd, too. We catch up as we scan the room, pretending that we're there to gal pal when it's obvious we're here to meet guys. If we really wanted to talk, we'd do lunch or go for a power walk.

Next to us are a pair of elder statesmen. They must be close to fifty, or even older. Divorcées, if I had to guess, from the way they're looking around, not talking to one another. Or married guys in search of a little on the side. I'm not attracted to men that age, and although my goal is to marry money, I'm not about to force myself into anything that doesn't feel right on a physical level. I'm not that desperate. I'll never be that desperate.

Lucy and I catch each other up on our happenings as we sip our cocktails and try not to look too available. She tells me about her latest case, a supposed whistleblower who it turns out was embezzling from his company and is now facing criminal charges. We pass the time, but my heart's not in it. I'm tired, and I think about reviving my online dating profile. I needed a break, but looking at the drink prices, a monthly subscription probably offers more bang for the buck.

I'm about to tell Lucy we should call it a night when I notice a guy standing in the corner, checking me out. He's alone, it seems. Wearing a suit and tie, which makes him stand out—in a good way. Frankly, I'm not a big fan of the dressing down trend. His dark gray suit jacket hangs perfectly on his broad shoulders, obviously tailor-made. A blue-and-white-striped tie sits on a starched white collared shirt. His face is serious and symmetrical. Handsome—and young enough for me.

I turn away, not wanting to make it obvious that I'm interested in him. Maybe he's not looking at me, in particular. The older guys next to me ask if they can buy us a drink, but I respectfully decline, although the drinks are so expensive here, I'll probably only be able to have two over the course of the evening.

Turning back to Lucy, I see that she's busy chatting with the guy next to her, so I sneak a glance back in Suit Guy's direction. His pressed lips curl up to a smile, letting me know that he knows I'm interested. He starts strolling in my direction, and I feel a little flutter in my stomach.

At least I think he's coming toward me, but now I can't see him through the crowd. After a few minutes, I spot him talking to one of the giggly girls. She's holding him by the arm, and his back is to me. It seems he's been intercepted. If he's looking for a hook-up, she's probably a better bet. Those days are over for me.

Oh well.

Lucy asks me if I want another drink.

I tell her I'm not sure.

A tap on my shoulder pulls my attention from her.

"I'd like to get that for you," a voice says as I turn around.

Suit Guy has a faint accent.

European.

Probably German, which explains the suit and tie.

"I'm Stefan," he says.

Well, I'll let him buy me a drink, but this isn't going to be the man of my dreams. I'm not about to play tour guide for some foreign guy looking for an escort during his business trip. But still, he seems nice enough, so I say yes to the drink.

"I'm Erin," I say. "And this is my friend Lucy."

When he smiles, his stoic exterior softens. I have to admit, Stefan is having an effect on me, in spite of myself. It's a little noisy in the bar now, and we have to strain to carry on a conversation. Lucy busies herself talking to the guy next to her, although I'm pretty sure she's not interested in him. She's a good wing woman.

Stefan keeps the focus on me, asking me questions about myself. I'm very selective about what I disclose in these kinds of situations. I work in marketing, I say, keeping it short and sweet.

If he asks, I'll reveal that I attended an exclusive private high school, followed by a prestigious liberal arts college for undergrad. I won't disclose that I was a scholarship student at both institutions. Erin Donovan, daughter of Mary Donovan, a single mother who worked two jobs that barely covered our rent.

But he doesn't ask much about my past. Rather, he asks me what I like to do. I tell him I'm more of an indoor cat, preferring museums and gallery openings to hikes and nature adventures. He smiles at this. A slightly crooked smile that makes him look less serious, more fun.

Up close, he's even more handsome than he was from far away. His twinkly eyes are dark hazel with a hint of blue, or perhaps that's the overhead light bouncing off my dress. I think he has the kind of eyes that change color depending on the setting. His jaw is square, his face angular and strong. Lips full, but not too full, and totally kissable.

Too bad he's not from here.

Stefan is a tad cagey about himself, not really answering my question when I ask what he does. "I'm in commodities," he says.

Is he a trader? Does he own an oil rig? Is he intentionally being vague to seem more intriguing? Whatever it is, it's working. The second champagne cocktail is loosening me up, and I can't believe I'm actually considering a one-night stand with this guy. Even though he's not marriage material, it's been months since my last relationship, and I have to admit, I miss the feel of a man's hands on my body. He smells good, too. A hint of aftershave mixed with man scent.

"Where do you live?" I ask, expecting something like Hamburg, Brussels, or Zurich.

"The Hamptons," he says. "Would you like to get out of here and grab some dinner? My driver's outside."

My eyes widen, and he gives me that closed-lip smile again. I try hard to dampen my enthusiasm, but I fail miserably. A giddy grin spreads up my face. He knows I'm going to say yes and so do I, even though the guy could be a serial killer, for all I know.

"Sure," I say. "I'd love to have dinner with you. But why don't we stay here and get a table? I'm not in the habit of getting into cars with strangers."

"Fair enough," Stefan says. "But we're not going to be strangers for very long."

TWO
ERIN

Warning bells blare in my head like a five-alarm fire. We've had three dates so far, and this seems too good to be true, even for an optimist like me. A single, rich, good-looking guy walks into a bar, spots me, and sweeps me off my feet. It's not like I have low self-esteem. I'm very attractive. Educated. But still. This happens here in Manhattan like…never. Just watch a few episodes of *Sex and the City,* and you'll see. It took basically the entire series for Carrie to get Big to commit, and he wasn't even that rich. There has to be a catch.

Three dates over the last two weeks, and believe it or not, so far we've only kissed a little, and that wasn't until the third date. That has me feeling a little suspicious, and I could kick myself for being so jaded. Maybe he's simply a gentleman. Or maybe he's the kind of guy who likes to take it slow. Do those guys actually exist? He's only in his mid-thirties. Perhaps he's married. Or seeing other women. None of it makes sense to me, unless I consider that maybe, just maybe, this is for real.

Which is hard for me. My mother worked at the

Cosmopolitan Club, one of the most exclusive private clubs in the city, on the Upper East Side. She was privy to all the gossip and intrigue of the one-percenters. More like the one-tenth of one-percenters, at a club like that. She filled my head with stories of infidelity, prenups, controlling marriages, unhappiness, a desperation for more that leads to an inability to appreciate what you have. And even the occasional suicide, the inevitable result of the constant pressure to keep up with the Joneses.

That was her way of trying to make me feel good about my humble origins, which was never going to be good enough to me, no matter how many cautionary tales she told me. And now that I have a chance at the kind of life I've always dreamed of, I have to fight the voice inside my head telling me it's some kind of trick, that this can't really be happening to me.

My initial thought was that it was a green card issue. He's foreign, and he needs to find someone to marry him so he can stay in the country, and that's why he's trying to fast-track this relationship with me. But he's got dual citizenship, he told me on our last date. Germany and the United States. He grew up dividing his time between Switzerland and New York, which is why his English is so good, not quite like a native speaker but close. And that faint, sexy accent adds an aura of mystery, like I'm stuck inside a James Bond movie.

Tonight is our fourth date. We had three in a row, and then he said he'd be busy for a week or two. He was very cryptic about what that meant, or why he couldn't see me. He keeps an apartment in the city, or so he said, but I haven't been there yet. If he went out of town, he didn't mention it to me. It's the beginning of summer now, so maybe he's staying in the Hamptons? For nearly a week, I thought he ghosted me. I didn't text him, given the fact that he said he'd be busy. Plus, I have a life; I don't need to revolve mine around him. And playing hard to get is never a bad idea.

But who am I kidding? I was thrilled when I got a text from him on day four, last Wednesday, asking me for a date on Friday of the following week, this coming Friday. That made me feel better. We had plans. And he was willing to commit to them. Then I got an intriguing text on the weekend we didn't see each other, the first weekend without a date since we'd met.

> Behaving yourself?

I responded:

> That depends. Are you?

It took him two days to text me again, and I was afraid he'd taken it the wrong way. But then a few days ago, he texted me the address of the restaurant we're meeting at for dinner. He offered to have his driver pick me up, but I said I'd meet him there. I still haven't given him my address. Then I got three more words:

> See you there.

No mention of his previous query, or my response. Interesting.

CATCHING LUCY'S EYE, standing across 59th Street from The Plaza Hotel, I wave at her. We're doing a power walk around Central Park, taking a little midday break. She needs to fill me in on what she's found out about Stefan. Being a criminal defense attorney, she has access to databases and information I don't. And an investigator who can dig up dirt on pretty much anyone. I check my phone for messages as she waits for the light to change and crosses over toward me.

I let out a sigh.

No more texts from Stefan.

"Hey, girl," Lucy says upon arrival. "Ring on that finger yet?"

I roll my eyes. She's the opposite of me. Says she doesn't need a man in her life. She's got an on-again, off-again romance with a federal prosecutor who works in the Southern District, and they both seem content to keep it business casual. But Lucy doesn't understand how it is for people like me. She wasn't at Cornwell Prep on a scholarship. And while she doesn't have a building with her name on it or anything, she has the kind of parents who could afford the sixty grand tuition, and then some.

"How far should we go?" I ask, ignoring her little dig.

"I've only got about forty-five minutes, and even that's pushing it. Got a meeting this afternoon with a rich white-collar criminal, my favorite kind. I shouldn't even be taking a lunch."

"Let's not venture too far in," I say.

Central Park is the kind of place where you can get turned around if you don't pay attention, and end up walking a lot more than you planned. The paths meander around, and I have no sense of direction, especially when I'm engrossed in conversation.

We head in and shift to the east, and I stop at a food cart to get a warm, salty pretzel and bottle of water, which kind of defeats the power walk; or maybe they balance each other out. I couldn't resist the savory smell. And although they're out of fashion these days, I love my carbs.

"So, what have you uncovered about Stefan Ziegler?" I ask, taking a bite of my pretzel.

"Stefan Ziegler is a curious one," she says.

"How so?" I ask.

"There's just not a lot on him, aside from the LinkedIn profile you've already sent me. Someone with that light of an internet presence has usually had themselves scrubbed."

I know a little about this process, but I ask her for more detail. She explains that there are reasonably priced services that can do a pretty good job of deleting basic information, like addresses and phone numbers. But to be as much of a ghost as Stefan Ziegler is, Lucy informs me, costs a great deal more.

"It might mean nothing. Lots of wealthy people do that to protect themselves and their privacy. But it can also be a red flag."

I nod.

A red flag.

Of course.

"He's too good to be true. I knew it," I say.

"Erin. Did you ever think that maybe, just maybe, you're giving these men in your life too much power over your happiness? You don't need a man to live the life you want."

I don't push back. She'll never understand, because Lucy

has a man in her life. A father, with a lot of money. And a mother who could volunteer at our prep school, help with college applications, and shop for expensive prom dresses. My father died when I was way too young, leaving my mother and me struggling and heartbroken.

I don't point this out. Nor do I point out that, although Lucy makes good money, she never would have been able to purchase a two-bedroom condo in a doorman building in Chelsea without the hefty down payment her parents gifted her. Not to mention that they picked up the tab for law school. I still have debt from my undergrad student loans—which weren't really used for my tuition because I had a scholarship—just for life. Law school would have been out of the question for me.

Instead, I change the subject. "Speaking of men, how's the booty call lifestyle working out for you?"

She smirks. "Just fine, thank you for asking."

Lucy and Justin Peterson, the prosecutor from the Southern District, have an arrangement of sorts, and she says it works for them.

Good for her.

But women like me, given the glass ceiling and my pile of debt, we're looking for more than just a fuck buddy. And right now, I have a date with Stefan Ziegler lined up for tonight. He might be the man of my dreams—or he might be the head of a notorious international crime syndicate. But at least I have a date this weekend.

And she doesn't.

We finish our walk, avoiding any controversial topics, and she promises me she'll keep digging and get back to me.

"If you go back to his place tonight," she adds, "text me the address, just in case."

"I'm not planning on it, but yeah, will do."
"Plans change," she says.
Indeed, they do.

THREE
ERIN

We meet at the restaurant he picked for us on the Lower East Side. Italian, which is my favorite. I wonder if he knows this. Unlike Stefan, I'm pretty out there with my social media. The kind of person who posts pics of my favorite meals, or my favorite walks. Or all of my favorite places to go. Come to think of it, I'd be easy to stalk. Maybe I should be a little more discriminating about what I post.

Stefan's waiting for me when I arrive, leaning on his town car, arms folded as if he owns the street, his driver taking up the space in front of the restaurant although it's a no-standing zone. He's in a suit again, a black one this time with a light blue collared shirt and a dark gray tie.

"Erin," he says. "You look amazing."

Expecting a smile, the corners of my mouth lift up to meet his. But he doesn't smile. He simply stares at me with his arms folded, as if he's appraising a painting or an artifact rather than greeting a human being.

I'm dressed in red tonight, a shorter dress with a little more of a plunge in the neckline, but still classy and respectable. Normally, I dress down on dates, especially going into the weekend. Jeans and a blouse, or maybe a short skirt and a jeans jacket. But he's so formal, I felt like he might take it as a sign of disrespect if I showed up like that.

He takes my hand, and he actually kisses the back of it, like something out of a Disney movie. Opening the passenger door, he barks something to the driver and shuts it behind us as the driver takes off. It dawns on me that if I'm going to be in a relationship with this guy, I need to learn some German.

"I'm sorry I haven't been more available," he says.

"It's fine," I say. "I've been busy, too." Which is, of course, not true. I've been exactly the same amount of busy as I always am, which is not too busy to go on a date with a guy like him.

We head inside, and the maître d' greets him like he's Secretary of State.

"Come right this way, Mr. Ziegler," he says.

Soon, we're settled in at the best table in the house, big enough for four but set for two, tucked away in a little alcove that gives us some privacy. His eyes are hazel, I notice, and his light brown hair seems to have gotten a trim since the last time I saw him. It's straight and close-cropped, framing a clean-shaven face, with a dusting of stubble attempting to poke through its chiseled ivory surface. I bet he's a neat freak.

At first, the conversation is a bit stilted, and I wonder if this is going to fizzle out. What I really want to ask is *where were you for the last two weeks?* Of course, I don't pry. He's not my boyfriend, and I'd be put off if he asked me something like that. But then, I wouldn't be so cryptic about where I'd been.

We got the basics out of the way on our first date. His

father lives in Germany now, his mother is deceased. But the family went back and forth between New York and Europe while he was growing up; his mother and father, Stefan and his younger brother.

Stefan attended boarding school in Switzerland, where English was the *lingua franca*. On our first date, I told him I was from New York and that I attended Cornwell Prep, a private school in the city, but I didn't tell him where in New York I grew up, or how I paid for it.

And now we're sort of stuck. We were getting somewhere, but I feel like we're starting to go backward. We sound more like acquaintances rather than two people on the brink of being lovers, so I throw him a curveball.

"Tell me something about yourself that you've never told anyone," I say, my chin resting gently on my fist as I gaze at him.

Stefan blows out a breath. "Well now, that's a dangerous question to ask a relative stranger, don't you think? What if I'm a serial killer?"

"You said we wouldn't be strangers for very long," I remind him, "and it's been pretty long."

I ignore his comment about being a serial killer. I doubt a real serial killer would joke about being one, so it actually makes me feel better about him. It's the first time he's hinted at a sense of humor. I'd like to see more of that.

The corners of his mouth lift. Not quite a smile, but almost. "You have a point. I did say that. Okay. Something I've never told anyone..." He takes a sip of his wine and purses his lips, an aristocratic air about him now.

"It doesn't need to be something major. Just something little that you're willing to share. Come on," I say. "It'll be fun. I promise."

Stefan looks away, and then back at me. "I hate caviar," he says.

"But you eat it anyway?" I ask.

He shrugs. "Everyone seems to love it, so I pretend."

And now we're getting somewhere.

"Your turn," he says.

This is harder than I thought it would be. My big secrets I'm not ready to share, and I don't really have many little ones. I take a sip of wine as we regard each other from across the table, the candlelight flickering between us. After a few minutes, I respond.

"My whole life, I've felt like a fraud," I confess.

Stefan tilts his head to one side, his brow furrowed. "Care to explain?" he asks.

"Not really," I reply.

I turn from him, my downcast eyes letting him know that I'm afraid I've gone too far. My balled fists sit on the tabletop, my nails digging into my flesh. I've allowed myself to be vulnerable with him, and it's put my stomach in knots.

The waiter comes over with our salads like a ninja, slipping them onto the tabletop and refilling our wine glasses before he departs, barely disturbing our prolonged silence.

Stefan reaches over and brushes my cheek with his fingertips, then he puts his hands on mine. Under the warmth of his touch, my hands unfurl. The energy between us has shifted now, and I already know from the look in his eyes we're no longer strangers.

We'll be sharing a bed tonight, of that much I'm certain.

Which one remains to be seen.

FOUR

ERIN

I poke my head out from under the sheets. The faint glow of the soon-to-be-rising sun illuminates the room, just enough to get my bearings. Turning my head to the left, I see Stefan's back is to me. He's curled over on his side, almost an arm's-length away. I remember falling asleep in his arms, and I wonder if he moved away in his sleep, or if he extracted himself from me after I drifted off.

The night comes rushing back to me as I watch the breath go in and out of his bare back, which is smooth and hairless, very pleasant to the touch. He's fit but slim, like a classic movie star from the fifties. The dinner itself is more of a blur. I ate, but I hardly tasted my food. Because from the moment we shared a bit of our real selves with each other, all we wanted to do was rip each other's clothes off. It was just a question of where it would happen.

I knew it would be safer for me to go to my place, but my apartment is on the small side, and it felt intimidating to bring a guy like Stefan back to it. It's not as small as some apartments, because I have a deal. It's rent-controlled, because I secretly sublet it from my great-aunt who's moved to a long-term care facility.

I fessed up to Stefan about my humble origins, so at least that's out of the way. He didn't seem too surprised, and I figure he probably did some background research on me, which is fair enough. I did the same on him, although I'm much more of an open book. When I revealed that I'd gotten myself through prep school and undergrad on a combination of academic, sports, and need-based scholarships and grants, he asked me what sport.

"Swimming," I said. "I was a competitive swimmer, from a young age."

I grew up in Bay Ridge, a working-class section of Brooklyn, not far from Coney Island and Brighton Beach. We weren't dirt poor or anything, at least not at first. We could afford the YMCA, which is where I learned to swim. But I told him I always loved the ocean.

"Do you swim anymore?" he asked.

"No," I said.

He asked why. I explained that in Manhattan, it's very expensive to get access to a decent pool. And plus, it's not the easiest thing to do on a lunch break or after work. I power walk for exercise now, I told him, but I miss swimming.

"Well, then, you should swim. We'll pick up your things, go to my house in the Hamptons tonight, and you can stay the weekend if you want. I've got a heated pool you can use for now. It's a little cold for an ocean swim, but it'll warm up before too long."

Was he actually suggesting that our romance would last into the summer season? This was the holy grail. A summer weekend escape in the Hamptons. Even if this relationship blew up in my face and left me heartbroken, I decided it was worth the risk.

Stefan assured me I could have my own suite at his house. He made it sound all innocent, which was nice. But when we got inside, it didn't go like that. Still, when he made his move, he stopped to ask if I was sure.

I was sure.

In bed, he touched me in all the right places, made all the right moves. Said all the right things. But it felt as if he was holding back a little, like there was a side of him that he wasn't quite ready to show. I'm not sure why I got that vibe. Maybe it was the way he grabbed my wrist in the beginning, his eyes filled with hungry passion, pinning my arm to the sheets, as if he needed me then and there.

But then he released his grip and trailed his hand along the curve of my body, slowing it down. I thought it would speed back up again, but it stayed pretty tame, although it was satisfying and surprisingly romantic. Truthfully, I wouldn't have minded if it got a little wilder, but we've got time for that.

We stopped by my apartment before we left the city to grab a bag, and I let him come up to see it. He made no comments about it either way, as if it was exactly as he'd suspected, which furthered my suspicions that he already knew where I lived, and that he'd done his homework on me.

When we arrived last night, I texted the address to Lucy, as promised, just in case I went missing and wound up locked in his basement; although I'm not sure there even is a basement at this house. But I figure if he was going to kidnap me and lock me in a secret room, he'd have done so already. And why would he do that with someone he was seen with on four occasions? Still, it's always best to let someone know your whereabouts with a new romance. And if anyone could get to the bottom of a missing person's case, it's Lucy Chang.

Slipping out of bed, I grab his shirt from last night, slide my arms in, and wrap it around me. It smells of him, and that makes me smile. Outside the bedroom window, the water sparkles under the morning sun.

The architecture is modern, with large wall-to-ceiling windows that drink in the natural beauty. Not overly large. Not a mansion or anything. But tasteful and stylish and, as I'd imagined, impeccably neat and tidy. Although the style and furnishings are modern, the art on the walls is more traditional. Landscapes and a family portrait, and not a hint of anything abstract or trendy, which doesn't surprise me. He's got an Old-World-European air about him.

I'd never heard of this area before last night, but when he told me the address, I looked it up. I discovered that Bayview Point is an artsy section of Southampton, on the northern shore of the island, fronting the Long Island Sound.

I could get used to this.

"Hey," he says.

I turn to see a rumpled Stefan, looking adorable. "Hey, sleepyhead," I reply.

"Says the woman who wore me out last night."

"Don't be such a baby."

"So, you said you didn't like the outdoors. We've got a few galleries and museums in town. Maybe after breakfast we could—"

"Oh, no," I say. "The beach is an exception. I'm not big on the mountains or the woods, or roughing it. But this? This is... spectacular."

Hopping back into bed, he reaches for me. Tingles shoot through me like a charge of electricity. The peaceful ambiance outside our love nest juxtaposed with the rush of new love is overwhelming, and I want him. Badly. We start to kiss, and it moves into a heavy make-out session. His hand slides up my thigh. It's about to get spicy when his phone buzzes and his hand stops.

It must be a reflex.

He's not going to stop and answer his phone, is he?

To my utter surprise, Stefan holds up a finger to me and reaches for his cell. Then he answers it, hops out of bed, and dashes out of the room in his boxers.

I sit up, shocked out of my mind.

What could be so important as to derail a man who's on the verge of getting laid?

It must be something pressing, though. Because even from two rooms away, I can hear him shouting into the phone. His tone is harsh. Brusque. And I can't understand a word he's saying, because he's speaking German. Maybe that's just the way that language sounds and he's not that angry? I doubt it.

I don't like this. I don't like it at all. It makes me feel very vulnerable, like he's got a big advantage over me. He can understand everything I'm saying, to everyone. And I can't do the same with him. That needs to change.

After a bit, Stefan returns. He apologizes, and I almost feel like rejecting him, just on principle. But when I look into his eyes, I see him longing for me. If anything, the little delay seems to have made him want me more.

So I give in.

And this time, he doesn't hold back.

AFTER OUR MORNING ROMP, Stefan heads to his dresser, pulls out dress shorts and a polo shirt, and puts them on. I follow suit, grabbing my yellow polka-dot sundress and slipping it over my head. It seems a little premature, since we haven't showered, and a little formal, since it's only the two of us. Maybe it's a European thing.

We head into the kitchen to get some coffee. It's a state-of-the-art chef's kitchen, gleaming and white, but I'm not sure if that means he likes to cook or if that's just status quo for a home like this. I guess he's not wealthy enough to have a private chef or a housekeeper. I did spot a small guesthouse out by the pool, which could be a maid's quarters, but this isn't an estate or anything, and if it weren't for the location, it would not be a multi-million-dollar house.

But this is Southampton, one of the most expensive zip codes in the country, and I have to pinch myself that I'm even here, standing in his kitchen, looking out at the pool and the tranquil sea rippling in the distance.

"I can whip us up some omelets," I offer. "Or whatever you like to eat."

"Don't be silly. You're my guest. What do you like for breakfast?" he asks.

I'm a guest, not a girlfriend.

Good to know.

"I'm not a big breakfast eater, truthfully. Just coffee, and maybe toast or some fruit? I'm more of a lunch person." I shrug.

He nods. "Me too. Let's get something in our stomachs and go for a swim. Then I'll take you out for lunch. That is, unless you have somewhere else to be."

Stefan smirks, like he thinks I wouldn't dare turn him down, and I wonder if I should make myself less available.

"I have something tomorrow," I lie. "But today, I'm pretty open."

He asks me what I want for coffee, and the number of options makes my head spin. He's got a cappuccino machine, a French press, and some other contraption I've never seen before, along with various flavors and types of milk. Soy. Almond. Regular.

"A cappuccino, with regular milk," I say.

Stefan pops a few slices of bread in the toaster, pulls some Greek yogurt and berries out of the fridge, and sets up a continental breakfast on the island countertop. It's gleaming white with faint sparkles, probably quartzite, if I had to guess. There's a formal dining room, but it seems as if we're staying here to eat, which is fine with me. It feels comfortable. Natural.

Stefan pats his shorts pocket. "I need to go grab my phone."

I sit with my coffee, admiring the lovely view of the pool and cabana, with the bay glimmering in the distance.

"Well, good morning to you," a voice behind me says.

My head whips around to see a man, about Stefan's age, with sandy brown hair, dressed in gym shorts and a tank top, his body glistening with sweat. I assume he's just worked out, and that's clearly a regular thing for him. His hair seems a bit contrived, like he gelled it a little to give it a faux bedhead look.

"Um... good morning," I say, my eyes wide and my mind reeling.

Is this why Stefan got dressed?

Who is this guy?

Is he a guest?

Is he the help?

No, he most certainly is not the help, or he would have addressed me in a different way, or not at all. Plus, the look on his face is too cheeky to be a hired hand. And then I notice something else, and my under-caffeinated mind struggles to process everything I'm seeing.

Stefan returns and takes in the situation.

I'm hoping he'll clear things up for me and offer some kind of explanation.

"Oh, I see you've met my brother, Tanner."

His brother?

"Your half brother," Tanner says, without any hint of an accent.

"You didn't tell me your brother lived with you," I say.

Stefan rolls his eyes. "It's temporary," he says.

Tanner laughs as I scan his frame again, still a bit gobsmacked. His tank top shows off well-defined biceps. Tight gym shorts hug his sculpted thighs. But my eyes rest on his lower legs, which bulge out like bowling pins from a pair of knobby knees. And nobody seems to want to address the giant, life-sized elephant in the room:

Tanner is wearing an ankle monitor.

I peer out from the guesthouse window and see a blonde woman with Stefan, holding a coffee mug and walking toward the pool.

My stomach lurches.

Is that...

No. For a minute there, I thought Amelia was back.

This must be a new one.

She's wearing a sundress, and they look as if they might sit out by the pool for a while. This isn't good. It's not good at all. I can't be seen here. How long will she stay? I need to get back home.

Blonde Girl is standing with her arms folded, facing Stefan with a quizzical look on her face. Stefan's back is to me, so I can't see his expression, but I assume he's trying to explain to her about Tanner and why he's wearing an ankle monitor.

Why did that idiot have to go and get the "good coffee" from the main house? Sometimes I want to bean Tanner over the head, just to knock some sense into him. But that would probably make it even worse. He's exasperating sometimes.

Stefan puts an arm on Blonde Girl's shoulder, brushes the hair back from her face, and kisses her. I know what that means. He's into her. Guys don't do that to one-night stands. She's his type, too. Busty and fertile with child-bearing hips, like a German milkmaid.

Just like the last one.

Tanner comes out the back door of the main house with his designer coffee. I hope he scalds himself with it. I move to the side so I won't be spotted when he enters.

He opens the door, about to greet me.

My eyes widen.

"*Shhh....*" I command.

With his floppy hair and lopsided grin, Tanner's like a golden retriever. He comes bounding up to me and gives me a wet kiss, and he actually does spill his coffee a little.

"Ouch," he says.

"Maybe put that down first?" I offer.

He nods, laughing at himself. "Yeah, good call, babe."

I shake my head and smile. It's hard to stay mad at a golden retriever.

Tanner is a work in progress. A diamond in the rough, if you will. He's got the body of an adonis, the maturity of a college freshman, and the impulse control of a toddler. But he has a way of seizing what he wants, and what he wants these days is me. I have to admit, it's a turn-on, after the last few years with my balding, middle-aged husband who barely touches me anymore.

"Who the hell is she?" I ask.

"Erin Donovan," he says, as if that explains everything.

And once again, I feel like bashing him over the head.

I roll my eyes. "No, Tanner. I mean, is she a girlfriend? Is she a one-night stand? I thought you said he was still getting over the last one."

Tanner shrugs. "We're not exactly close, Maddie. I know as much as you do. He barely tolerates having me here. And can you stop being such a bitch?"

I take a deep breath.

Yes, I can be bitchy. It goes with the territory. I should tone it down a little. "Sorry, hon. I'm just stressed. I have to get home. Jeremy's not stupid. You need to distract them so I can get out of here," I say.

"Oh, that's hot. Like we're a spy couple." Tanner grabs me by the shoulders. He runs his hand up my inner thigh and flashes me a sexy grin. "We've got time for a quicky, babe."

I start to tingle in all the right places.

I want to.

Really, I do.

But one of us has to be practical.

Still, I have to marvel at his stamina.

Will I ever wear him out?

"Down, boy," I tell him. "Later. There's too much at stake. I have to get home. Jeremy knows how long my power walks last."

We land on a plan, and I placate Tanner with an offer to come back later, once Stefan and the milkmaid are out of the house. He kisses me goodbye, and I almost give in.

Almost.

But not quite.

For this to work, Tanner needs to get them to look in the

opposite direction of the guest house for a few minutes, so I can sneak out the back and dodge the cameras.

We know the drill. We've been at it for a while now.

It's a stupid plan. A very stupid plan, but it just might work. So, I hold my breath and hope for the best. Because if anyone can pull off a plan this stupid, it's Tanner.

SIX

ERIN

"Bombs away!"

Tanner?

My eyes dart toward the sound of his voice.

Stefan's head whips around as Tanner sprints toward the infinity pool like a bat out of hell.

Oh my God.

Is he naked?

My eyes follow him as he passes us, his butt cheeks bouncing in the wind as he speeds across the pavers.

"No!" Stefan cries out. "You can't get it wet!"

Inches before he's about to reach the pool's edge, Tanner screeches to a halt.

"Shit, that's right, bro," he says.

Tanner turns back toward us and starts to strut over. Reflexively, I shield my eyes, but not before noticing that he's got on some kind of thong bathing suit. It's tan, almost the color of his skin. Thankfully, it covers his whatsis.

I remove my hand. Still, I'm having trouble with the visual. He's ripped, that's for sure. More ripped than Stefan, and Tanner seems proud of that fact, sticking out his chest like he's about to bump Stefan with it. In a physical brawl, Stefan wouldn't stand a chance.

Stefan shakes his head. "What am I going to do with you?"

Tanner shrugs. "I forgot," Tanner says. "Man, this summer's gonna *suck*."

"It's better than spending it in prison," Stefan points out.

"This whole thing is bullshit," Tanner says. "I never should have taken the deal."

"Let's not do this now," Stefan says.

I got the basics from Stefan, before we were interrupted. Tanner is his half brother, and he's two years older than Stefan. Same father, different mothers, but I didn't get much, or really any detail about that. Tanner is under house arrest, serving a six-month sentence for trying to pass off a forgery as a valuable piece of modern art. He's got a little less than four months left of his sentence. Stefan claims he took Tanner under his wing and tried to give him a job, but it didn't work out very well.

Obviously.

"Are you an art dealer?" I asked Stefan.

"Sort of. My business is complicated," he said.

And that was that.

It seems pretty clear that he doesn't want to tell me much about what he does, and we're not really at the place where I can be demanding.

I'm a guest, after all.

Not a girlfriend.

I knew it was too good to be true.

Tanner excuses himself and goes back to his guest house. Stefan asks if I'd like to go for a swim. I tell him maybe later.

Something about Tanner makes me uncomfortable, and I'm not sure I care to be so exposed in front of him just yet.

"How about we check out the bay?" he asks.

"Sure," I say. "Let me use the bathroom first."

But already my mother's warnings echo in my mind. Tanner is a criminal. Stefan is as cryptic as they come. Rich people have secrets, she told me once. Dangerous ones you're better off not knowing. It's a fair point, so I don't want to ask a lot of questions.

Instead, while I'm in the bathroom, I send off a text to Lucy with Tanner's name and ask her to do a little digging around on him.

Because Stefan's secrets are only dangerous for me if he knows that I know them.

STEFAN and I make our way to the water's edge. Stefan's house sits on a relatively small lot, but it's very close to the water. Peconic Bay, it's called. It's not suitable for swimming. The area is more marshy than sandy, with native grasses, cacti, and other shrubs. Mature trees shelter the property and make it feel private, but when we get down to the water, I can see that we're pretty close to the other houses. It's nice and peaceful here, and for some reason, I like that it's not so secluded.

Easier to escape, if it comes to that.

Then I shake my head, trying to stay positive. Art forgery isn't exactly attempted murder. And Tanner said he took a deal. Maybe he's innocent, taking the fall for someone. But he works for Stefan, so that wouldn't be good. I wipe that out of my mind as I try to enjoy the scenery and Stefan's company. Tanner will be around the entire summer, so already my romantic fantasies are tarnished at the edges. I need more information. Hopefully, Lucy can get me something.

"You're quiet," Stefan says.

"Just taking it all in," I reply, slipping off my sandals and dipping my toe in the water. It's not as cold as I thought it would be.

The silence fills the space between us, like a growing cancer.

"It's Tanner, isn't it?" he says.

"Um, no, I'm just..." I sigh. "Yeah," I confess. "It's Tanner."

"He's harmless, I promise. Tanner meant well, but he got duped. He's... excessively optimistic, and he believed the art he acquired was authentic. But if we went to trial, our family would have been dragged through the mud. It was easier all around to settle, given the cushy deal they offered him. He's from L.A., and he'll go back after he serves his time. Don't worry, Erin. It's all under control. It's only a few more months, and we'll have the place to ourselves."

This makes me feel a little better.

We start to stroll along the shoreline.

A woman waves to us from her back deck, posing like a fashion model with her back slightly curved and a hand on her hip.

"Hey, Stefan," she calls out in a singsong voice.

"Hi, Madison," he replies.

Madison has dark wavy hair, about shoulder-length. She looks about forty. Very fit, wearing yoga pants and a crop top. Not drop-dead gorgeous, but attractive with a kind of raw sex appeal; or maybe it's the way she's looking at Stefan. I wonder for a moment if something is going on between them.

She saunters over to us.

Her back is stick straight but there's a slight sway in her hips.

Stefan lets out a sigh, and I get the feeling he's not too thrilled about this.

"I'm Madison Bradford," she says upon arrival, dipping her hand toward me, as if I'm supposed to shake her fingertips.

"Erin Donovan," I say, ignoring the hand, which she promptly pulls away.

"For a moment there, I thought you were Amelia."

She glances toward Stefan and then back at me.

Who the hell is Amelia?

"Are you summering in the Hamptons?" she asks, crossing her arms.

Stefan intervenes. "Erin's a friend of mine," he says. "She's from the city, but I'm hoping to see more of her around here."

"I'm actually from Bay Ridge," I add. "But I live in the city now."

Stefan puts his arm around me, and Madison forces a smile.

"Madison?" A man calls out from her deck.

The man looks older than her, casually dressed in shorts and a polo shirt, probably close to fifty. Decent build, from what I can tell, but a little overweight. The receding hairline isn't flattering, coupled with his large forehead and sunken eyes.

"We have to go soon," he says.

"Coming, Jeremy," she shouts back. "Well, I need to get

going. Let's have coffee the next time you're around, Erin. I'd love to get to know you, since you're a friend of Stefan's. I could use some girl talk. And we gals have to stick together, right?"

"Right," I say with a smile. "I'll try to fit you into my... busy social schedule."

We share an awkward chuckle, then she turns from us and we get back to our walk.

Although she obviously has an agenda, Madison could be useful to me, so I plan to take her up on that coffee, since I'm going to be a regular here in the Hamptons. Because if anyone around here has the scoop on Stefan and Tanner and this bizarre situation, it's a woman like Madison Bradford.

Stefan's hoping to see more of me, he said, but I have to be careful not to seem so available, and I don't want to spend all our time here. I'm not too keen on being under a microscope, between his brother the felon and his nosy neighbor, and we need time alone to get to know each other. Thankfully, we've both got apartments in the city.

"The Hamptons are great," I say. "But there's nothing quite like Manhattan."

Stefan puts his arm around me. "You'll get used to it here," he says.

I find his confidence both infuriating and enticing.

Once we're out of view of the Bradfords, he stops walking and turns to me.

Softly, he caresses my cheek as he looks deep into my eyes. "You're not a fraud, Erin. You're the most real woman I've met in a very long time. Please don't change."

For a long moment, I stare into his haunting eyes as they pull me in, deeper and deeper. I want to believe what he's saying is real.

And why would he lie?
This is happening, I tell myself.
It's real.
He's for real.
My stomach does somersaults as I fall into the abyss.
He leans in and our mouths meet.
I melt into the kiss.
I'm a gonner.

SEVEN
ERIN

After our lunch and a quick tour of the town, Stefan and I returned to his place. He took me to a cute little spot on the marina with picnic tables draped with red-and-white-striped tablecloths where we ate fish sandwiches and drank iced tea. Nothing fancy, and I'm trying not to read too much into that.

I asked him about Amelia, and he said she was his last girlfriend. When I prodded him further about what happened to her, he looked at me like my question confused him.

"Nothing happened to her," he said. "We broke up."

He shrugged, and I didn't take it any further.

I have told him absolutely nothing about my previous relationship, or any of them for that matter, so I didn't press it any further. We're not at that kind of place, and he doesn't seem like the type who likes to rehash the past.

"What time do you have to be back in the city tomorrow?" he asks.

"I have lunch plans with a friend, so mid-morning?"

That's not even a lie anymore, because Lucy and I are

meeting. She's got some information that she needs to give me in person, which is intriguing yet unsettling.

He nods. "Maybe we should go back late this afternoon, so we don't hit traffic tomorrow."

I wonder if this means we aren't spending Saturday night together, and my stomach sinks. I probably shouldn't put all my eggs in his basket. Guys like him usually like to play the field. I need to manage my expectations.

But then I think about that kiss.

He's a little hot and cold.

Maybe it's a German thing?

"Why don't you go for that swim?" Stefan offers. "After all, that's why we came here, isn't it?"

Is he serious? I thought we came here to... well, you know.

It seems like he really wants me to go for a swim, though. It's not the first time he's asked me. Is he testing me? Does he think I'm lying about being a fast swimmer?

"Sure," I say. "And yes, I think going back this afternoon is a good plan." Partly I'm saying this because I don't want to seem too eager, and also because I don't like having Tanner here, spying on us. I'm dying to ask about the conditions of his plea deal. Does he have any latitude to leave the house, or is he stuck inside these walls for the next four months? I think sometimes they have a radius. But I don't want to ask, so I'm hoping Lucy's found something out.

"I'll swim with you," he says. "I could use some exercise."

We change into our suits and head out to the pool. I brought my red bikini, not my workout suit. Stefan's wearing navy swimming trunks, which surprises me. I thought Europeans wore Speedos.

"Last one in's a rotten egg," I call out with a smirk on my

face, leaving Stefan in the dust as I dive into the deep end with near-perfect form. The water is a temperate eighty-five degrees, if I had to guess. Saltwater filtration with no chlorine.

Heavenly.

Gliding through the water, my body takes over. I feel at one with the universe when I swim, my rhythmic strokes putting me in a kind of hypnotic trance, blocking everything else out, even Stefan. After about five minutes, I remember where I am and pop up.

Stefan is sitting on the pool's edge, his legs dangling in the water, watching me with a sexy grin on his face. "Well, hello there," he says.

"Sorry," I say. "It's been a while. I forgot how much I love this."

"It loves you, too," he says. "Watching you, it's... poetic."

Poetic? I wonder if that's a language issue. Nobody has ever described my swimming as poetic. Still, it's a compliment, so I'll take it.

"Come in," I say. "I'll race you."

I splash a little water at him.

Stefan's jaw stiffens.

"Sorry," I say, concerned for a moment that he might be too uptight for me.

"I'll bet you can't beat her," I hear Tanner say.

My head turns toward his voice.

And I realize the look on Stefan's face isn't for me, it's for his brother.

That's a relief, but it also makes me less enthused about spending a lot of time here this summer. Tanner obviously knows we're trying to have a date here, and he still came out of the guest quarters. Nobody's that clueless.

Maybe Tanner's intentionally trying to ruffle Stefan's feathers.

But why?

"We don't have to race," I offer.

Stefan hops into the pool. "I'm secure in my manhood," he says. "I've got nothing to prove."

"I'm just messing around with you, bro," Tanner says. "Sorry I bothered you two lovebirds. But I'm going a little stir crazy, being alone here so much of the time."

It dawns on me that the isolation could get to a person, being stuck alone in a house for six months, even at a luxury property like this, so I cut Tanner some slack. And it seems as if Stefan does, too.

"You can stay out here," Stefan says. "We're going back to the city soon, anyway."

"Oh man, I miss the city. I miss *my* city. I can't wait to get back to L.A.," Tanner says.

This makes me feel better.

Tanner won't be here forever.

We decide to do a little race, just for fun. And so I don't make things worse between Tanner and Stefan, I decide I'll let Stefan win.

"Ten laps," Tanner says.

We nod and take our places.

Tanner positions himself at the starting line.

"On your marks. Get set. Go!"

Once we get going, it's impossible to tell who is winning, so I abandon that idea of letting Stefan win and just go for it, as if I'm in a real race.

When I finish my last lap and grab the pool's edge, I whip around and see Stefan swimming in my direction. His stroke isn't bad, but he wastes energy pulling himself too far out of the water, a common mistake. I didn't win by that much, and after all, swimming is my thing, so I should be good at it.

Stefan seems amused and not the least bit upset that I've beaten him.

"Well done," he says.

I shrug and explain to him about his stroke. "If you adjusted that a little, you'd leave me in the dust. I don't have the upper body strength that you have."

"Well, maybe you can be my instructor this summer," he offers, then he looks at his watch. "I need to make a call. I'll be back in a few. Feel free to stay and enjoy your swim, Erin."

With that, he extracts himself, pulling himself up onto the ledge, stepping up, and wrapping a towel around his waist. He leaves me standing in the pool, with Tanner looking down at me.

After Stefan's out of earshot, Tanner says to me, "You should have let him win, Erin. My brother doesn't like to lose."

I feel a cold chill ripple through me, although I'm still catching my breath from the race. Trying not to read too much into it, I tell myself that Tanner's warning is nothing more than sibling rivalry. But then I flash back to Stefan shouting at people—in a language I don't understand—and wonder again what he was saying.

Tanner continues. "By the way, you beat him by three laps, but don't let on that you know that. For your own good," he says.

And then he turns from me to return to his quarters, leaving me standing in the water, speechless.

EIGHT

MADISON

Sunday morning is family time in the Bradford house. The nanny is off on the weekends, until later in the summer when the kids are off from school. The housekeeper makes herself scarce, staying in her quarters, because she has weekends off. The four of us stuff our faces with French toast or pancakes or waffles, and I try not to have a panic attack about the staggering amount of carbs we take in.

But it's once a week, and I'll burn it off. I've given up on Jeremy. At age seven, my son Oliver can afford it. But my daughter is approaching puberty and she's starting to put on some weight. I had that problem, too, so I'm trying to steer her in the right direction. My parents sent me to fat camp, and it was humiliating. Hopefully, we can keep it from getting that bad with Abby, but I don't want to give her a complex, either. Parenting is so hard.

Jeremy and I were happy once, and that seems like another lifetime most days. But on Sunday mornings, it almost feels like it did years ago, when we were young and in love. Well, I was young. He's nearly ten years older than me, but you know what I mean. The love was young, full of hope and possibilities. Now it's stale. Predictable. Boring. And even rude sometimes, the way Jeremy barks at me as if I'm another underling he gets to boss around rather than the mother of his children.

"Mom!" Oliver cries out. "You're burning it!"

Today it's pancakes, and oh crap, they are practically on fire. I shut off the burner and wave a rag at the smoke alarm, which, thankfully, hasn't started blaring yet.

Get your head in the game, Madison.

I've been rattled ever since yesterday, and that run-in with Stefan and his new squeeze. After we got back from Abby's tennis lesson and Oliver's soccer game yesterday, I checked in with Tanner to see if he found out anything more. He sent me a few cryptic texts that added up to nothing, and then he tried to get me to come over for another tryst. But I feel like Jeremy is getting suspicious, so I told him we'll need to wait until Monday, when Jeremy and Stefan are at work.

The new batch of pancakes survived, a little undercooked but still passable. I set them on the table with whipped cream, berries, and chocolate chips.

"Yikes," Jeremy says. "You trying to burn down the house and run off with the insurance money?"

I roll my eyes. "Very funny."

But see, these are the kinds of comments he's been making lately that make me think he's on to me. Little digs here and there, which I ignore.

Deny everything.

Once seated around the table, we laugh and joke and carry on like a normal family, or what I assume is a normal family, like the ones I saw on sitcoms. I grew up with old money, and there were certain expectations. Traditions, if you will, that I had to uphold.

It was a lot of pressure, and even marrying someone like Jeremy, who is more self-made, ruffled some feathers. Not that Jeremy was poor. He grew up in Ridgewood, an upscale suburb in New Jersey. Attended an Ivy League college. Got a job in finance and worked his way up. Truthfully, calling him self-made is a bit of a stretch; he had a pretty solid head start. But he wears the label like a badge of honor, rubbing it in my face from time to time, as if my interior design business, which I gave up years ago, was a gift from my parents.

It wasn't.

After a few years of marriage, he started to change.

Because here's the truth about families like mine with old money: we're running out of it. So now, the tables have turned. In the beginning, I had the upper hand, but not anymore. Jeremy's put me on a tight leash as far as spending, too. And now I want out. But it's not that easy. Neither of us could afford to live the way we want if we split our net worth. We're barely keeping up now. I needed something to make me feel alive again. Then I met Tanner.

It was supposed to be a fling, but then he started filling my head with ideas about the two of us, after he got his share of his family fortune. Nothing specific, just little comments here and there to keep me intrigued. Then he got arrested, and I started to realize that he wasn't going to be the answer to my problems.

And then it got even more complicated.

"Mom," Oliver says. "These aren't that bad!" He smiles, and with that missing front tooth, he's just too adorable. My heart melts.

I can't be that bad of a person if I love my kids this much, right?

"Thanks, sweetie," I say. "Abby, that's enough for now. Remember, it takes twenty minutes for your brain to realize that your stomach is full. And we want to go for a swim after, so don't get too stuffed."

My daughter nods, and I hope I'm not going to give her an eating disorder. Jeremy shoots me a look. We've been at odds over this. She's daddy's little girl, and in his eyes, she's perfect. And she is, of course. It's just that I'm a realist. Men can get away with being paunchy and still come off desirable to women decades younger than them. Just look at my husband, who is living proof. He's such a fucking hypocrite. And just when I was starting to feel bad about my affair, I remember why I started it, and I'm seething again.

With an excuse about needing to use the bathroom, I dash away from the table to check my burner phone. I can't believe I actually have a burner phone. It's so exciting, like I'm playing a part in a movie. Like it's not really me.

But if Jeremy caught me in bed with Tanner, what would he really do? Would he divorce me? I doubt it, for the same reason I won't divorce him, at least not right now. Maybe it would even make him more attentive. Give him a wake-up call. Lord knows he needs one.

Looking at Tanner's text, my stomach lurches, and Monday can't come soon enough:

Got news. Not good.

NINE
ERIN

Turns out, it's very handy to have a friend who is a defense attorney sleeping with a prosecutor in the Southern District. Lucy worked her magic, and she came to lunch armed with a virtual dossier on Tanner Wilkens. He's from New York originally, but moved to L.A. to surf and attend college, then dropped out. Before he came back here to work for Stefan, he was an aspiring model and actor who made his living as a bartender at a trendy restaurant.

Tanner grew up thinking his father was a mortician from Long Island named Tony Wilkens, now deceased. And survived by Tanner's mother, Millie Wilkens, who has since closed the business and retired in Vero Beach, Florida. No mention of when or how he found out that he was heir to a small fortune.

Yes, a small fortune. Because not only has Stefan made a name for himself here in the New York business world, he's also in line to inherit an old money estate in Germany, a few hours outside of Munich. Stefan's now the sole heir, or so it seems, because his younger brother died in a skiing accident a few years back, something Stefan neglected to tell me. Thinking back on what Tanner said when I was standing in the pool, I take a deep breath and ask a question I'm not sure I want to know the answer to.

"So, are you telling me that Tanner is a threat to Stefan's inheritance?"

I take a bite of my way-too-expensive salad. Lucy wanted to meet near Central Park, after her jog, and we opted for a casual bistro on the Upper East Side, but it's still thirty dollars for a salad. With a coffee and tip, I won't get out of here for under fifty bucks.

Lucy shrugs. "I don't have that kind of information. All I know is that Tanner tried to pass off a forgery at auction, and he got caught. The feds are watching Stefan and his business now. Art is only a part of your boy's business dealings. My advice is, proceed with caution."

Lucy picks at her salad and calls the waiter over. "Are these red onions?" she asks. "I specified no red onions."

"I think they're radishes," the waiter offers.

"Are you willing to chance that? And have me barf all over the table and sue this place?" she asks. "I'm highly allergic to red onions. I could *die*." She widens her eyes.

"I'll take care of it," he says, whisking her bowl away.

"You could die?" I smile and shake my head.

"It's possible," Lucy says. "And at these prices, they need to get it right."

She's not wrong about that, and I admire her gumption. Lucy Chang takes no crap from anyone, and I could stand to be a bit more like her.

She seems concerned about Stefan, and I am, too. Art

forgery is big business. I know this because I work for a public relations and marketing firm that serves the visual arts community, and I have to wonder now if meeting Stefan in that bar was actually a coincidence, or if he somehow targeted me. Maybe he thinks I could be useful to him.

It's estimated that over 50 percent of all art exhibited in homes and public spaces could be forgeries. But after the largest forgery scandal in the history of the art world over a decade ago, the scams seem to have slowed down.

As if reading my mind, Lucy continues. "Tanner may have been duped, as he claims. But it's notable that he tried to pass off a forgery of a relatively unknown artist's work. Not like that big scandal a decade ago, where the scammers went high profile, trying to pass off fake Pollocks and Rothkos. If someone were trying to test the waters, they'd go low profile. Much less likely to attract attention."

I let out a sigh.

Stefan seemed so genuine yesterday morning.

Am I this gullible?

"What should I do?" I ask Lucy.

"Well, see, here's the thing. Justin isn't usually so forthcoming about their cases. He told me all this because he wants me to ask you a favor."

My brow furrows. "A favor? What kind of favor?"

Lucy continues. "If you decide to keep seeing him, maybe you could keep an eye out for anything suspicious. Report back to Justin."

"You're asking me to spy on Stefan?"

"Not spy, Erin. Justin's not with the CIA. More like a... confidential informant."

"Are you crazy? No. I'm not doing that. What if he finds

out? If Stefan's a criminal, I'll be at risk. And if he's not, it'll ruin my relationship with him."

"Don't shoot the messenger, Erin. You're the one who wanted me to dig around in the first place, so I dug." She shrugs. "This is on you."

I sigh.

She's right.

"What would you do if you were me?" I ask.

"That depends. How do you feel about him?" she asks.

I think about the look in his eyes when he caressed my cheek and hear his words as clearly as if he were standing next to me.

You're the most real woman I've met in a very long time, Erin.

Please don't change.

"I think I'm falling in love with him," I confess. "It's not just the money, Lucy. I swear. There's a real connection between us. He's into me, I can tell. And I'm into him. I'd like to see where it goes."

"Then keep seeing him," Lucy says. "But I want you to memorize this number." She hands me a slip of paper. "It's a hotline of sorts. If you find yourself in any danger, call and use Justin's name. Stefan may very well be into you—and he also might be a notorious criminal. Those two things aren't mutually exclusive.

"And while art forgery isn't usually a violent crime, there's a lot of nasty stuff tied up in the art world these days. Money laundering for terrorists. Gun running. Until we know more about what we're dealing with, I'm warning you. Proceed with caution."

"GUTEN TAG," says a woman with a toothy smile and long braids, standing at the front of our table with a coffee in her hand. She could be Pippi Longstocking's grandmother.

She proceeds to chatter away in German, motioning to the seats around the table. The ad said this was a German immersion class, and she wasn't kidding. I've understood nothing since her greeting. I assume we are supposed to sit, but I look to my two other classmates for confirmation. One is an elderly man, the other a young woman; early twenties if I had to guess.

We shrug.

And then we sit.

"Das is gut," the instructor says as she claps for us, a smile mushrooming across her face. Her grin is so wide, she almost looks deformed. She tries German on us again and is met with blank stares. Thankfully, she switches to English, introduces herself as Heidi Mueller, then teaches us how to introduce ourselves in German. We go around the table and practice.

We're at a coffee shop. It's very noisy and hard to understand her. I suppose this is what I get for choosing a bargain-priced language class. Going around the table again, in English this time, we disclose why we are taking the class, at her request. It must be some kind of icebreaker she cooked up. At this rate, it will take forever to understand what Stefan's saying. I need a better plan. I've never been great at languages, and before I met him, I had zero interest in learning German. It's only slightly more than zero now.

The young woman whose name is Maya says she's going to Germany as an exchange student next semester, and she wants to learn to converse.

Heidi teaches her a few phrases that would be helpful for a student.

Where is my classroom?

What time does class begin?

Heidi explains that learning entire phrases is quicker, and she doesn't recommend spending a lot of time on grammar.

She moves on to the elderly man, who declined to give his name.

He reports that he's learning German because there's a man in his building who's a "Nazi bastard," and he wants to know what the guy is up to.

"I don't trust the Germans," he mutters. "Never did."

Heidi smiles and tries to persuade him that the real Nazis are all dead and buried.

Then he accuses her of being one and storms off.

My turn.

"I'm taking the class because I'm going on a business trip to Berlin," I lie.

There's no way I'm telling her about my romance.

Heidi teaches me a few business phrases.

Where is the conference room?

What time is our meeting?

Then she excuses herself to use the restroom.

Maya, the student, shows me an app she's been using.

"It's really great for understanding what people are saying," she says. "I listen to podcasts and YouTube videos in German and watch the words on my phone screen. My comprehension is getting much better. But I'd like to be able to converse. Go out to bars and all that," she says. "Make friends. But if you're only there for a short business meeting, it might work for you. Lots of people are using them these days. It's no big deal."

Genius.

"This is perfect for me, Maya," I say. "Thanks so much for telling me about it."

I don't care about conversing in German. In fact, I don't even want Stefan to know that I understand what he's saying. I'll put the app on my phone and the next time he rushes out to talk on his cell, I'll try to stand close enough so it can translate what he's saying.

Heidi returns, and I make up a story about a friend calling from the hospital with an emergency.

"Now you have private lesson!" Heidi says to Maya, with her mile-wide toothy smile.

She certainly is a happy individual. You can't fake that kind of enthusiasm. Maya looks equally pleased, and I leave the two of them, excited to use my newfound superpower the next time an opportunity presents itself.

I just hope I don't get caught.

When I get back to my apartment, I see a text from Stefan. It's very late in the day, and it's not exactly what I was hoping for.

It took all day for him to miss me enough to send a text?

> How's dinner on Tuesday?

I decide to ignore him for a while.

Stefan and I didn't spend Saturday night together. We ended up having an early dinner at his place in the Hamptons, and by the time we got back to the city, it was nearly eight o'clock in the evening. He saw me up to my apartment and then said he needed to get going. Then he gave me a peck on the lips, told me he'd be in touch, and took off.

Either Stefan's playing hard to get, or we're not in the place I thought we were. Truthfully, he's a little hot and cold, and two can play at that game.

But still, I'm an optimist.

So, I cue up some YouTube videos in German, open the translation app, and start honing my superpower, just in case this actually goes somewhere.

"So," I ask, tapping my foot on the travertine tile floor of Tanner's guesthouse, which truthfully is more like a pool house or a cabana. "What did you find out?"

Even as a maid's quarters, this would be considered substandard housing in Southampton, and I'm surprised he stays here instead of in the main house. I guess Stefan really is the asshole Tanner claims him to be.

Tanner has what appears to be a hopeful gleam in his eye, or maybe that's just the way he looks when he wants sex —which I put on hold until he gives me more information.

After he waves me over to the sink where he's filling up his water bottle, he utters one word, under his breath:

Pflichtteil.

"Huh? Is that supposed to mean something to me?" I ask, shaking my head.

I'm not delusional. I know that going from Jeremy to Tanner is like going from the proverbial fire to the frying pan. This was supposed to be a fling, after all. A little payback. Not my next step.

But if this isn't my next step, what is?

Tanner continues. "It's an old concept in German inheritance law, embedded in their contemporary law code. I'm entitled to a share of my father's estate, no matter what the will says. Not an equal share to Stefan, but the least he can give me is half of my fair share, which, since his mother and brother are dead, would amount to a quarter of everything my father owns. Doesn't matter if Stefan gets married, has a kid, or what."

"Isn't that a good thing?" I ask. "Why did you say the news isn't good?"

"Because there's a catch," he says. "I can be disinherited, under certain conditions."

"Like?"

Tanner presses his lips into a tight grimace. "Like a felony conviction," he replies.

Then he pounds the kitchen counter with his fist, hitting it so hard, my eyes almost see stars, but he doesn't flinch.

"Don't you see? That bastard set me up! He knows all about this provision."

Rubbing his hand, he paces around the living area. At first, I thought Tanner's suspicions about his brother stemmed from a combination of jealousy and paranoia, but now I'm not so sure.

"What does this mean? Are you cut off now?"

"From what I've read, in order for the courts to side with my father, it would need to be a longer prison sentence, a year or more. But you never know what the courts will do in a case like this. They have guidelines, not rules."

"Maybe you should consult with an attorney," I offer.

"No, not yet. I don't want my brother to know that I even

know about this. He'll find out. I don't want to end up like Reinhold."

Reinhold?

Stefan's younger brother?

"But Reinhold is... dead," I whisper.

His eyes widen. "Exactly."

"Are you suggesting that Stefan had something to do with Reinhold's death? He died in a skiing accident. There were witnesses, I'm sure."

"Right, that's what they say. But there was no autopsy. He was an expert skier and went barreling off a cliff. Stefan could have drugged him. Or tampered with his equipment. And remember Amelia? She practically fled from the Hamptons with no advance notice, right after she broke off the engagement. Don't you think that's odd? And where is she? No social media. No trace of her, anywhere."

The hairs on the back of my neck stand on end.

Does he suspect something?

"Stefan and Amelia broke up. Why wouldn't she leave town? Do you know more than you've told me?"

He shakes his head. "No. It's just a hunch."

"Tanner," I say. "This all seems very... unlikely. He'd have to be some kind of stone-cold psychopath. People would have seen through him by now. And if Stefan knows about the law, he wouldn't have told you to take the deal. You're doing six months' house arrest, and that's not enough to disinherit you, according to your own research."

Tanner glares at me. "Whose side are you on, Maddie? If I went to trial, I'd have been acquitted, or maybe they would have figured out he was in on it. Six months is better than nothing. I didn't know the painting was a fake. He set me up. I'm sure of it."

Then his face turns somber, the look of a wounded child. "I know most people will believe him over me. I'm the bastard love child my father never wanted. Stefan is the golden boy. But even you? Even you don't believe me? I thought we were in this together."

"It's not that simple, Tanner," I say.

He gazes out the window for a minute with a faraway look in his eyes.

Then he speaks, as much to himself as to me:

"I was happy once. Before all of this started. And sometimes I wish I never knew I was related to these people. It would be easier that way. But I do know. And it burns me up, thinking about the way that bastard used my mother and then tossed her aside. She deserves her fair share, too, and I'm the only one who can get it for her."

I let out a sigh. "I've never looked at it that way."

Tanner plops down on the love seat, and I take the spot next to him as he hangs his head in his hands. This situation can't be easy, and I feel for him. It's true that ignorance is bliss. If Tanner hadn't found out about his real father, he'd have nothing to be jealous or angry about.

Rubbing his shoulder, I try to offer him the support he needs. "I'm on your side, Tanner. And I think it's possible Stefan set you up for the art forgery to disinherit you. But to claim he murdered his own brother? Or that he's somehow done something to Amelia, or caused her to disappear? I'm sorry, but that's a bit of a stretch for me. If you really think that's the case, you might be safer in prison."

Tanner's head tilts to one side, as if he'd never considered that before. "You might have a point. But if I want to prove he set me up, I need to be here, keeping tabs on him. And I'm not letting Stefan off that easy. If he comes after me, I promise you it'll be the last thing he ever does."

With that, the wounded little boy look is replaced by a steely expression, part lust and part determination. His hand reaches between my legs and clamps on as if I'm a refuge in a storm. For what feels like forever, he keeps his hand perfectly still.

The heat courses through me until it's almost too much to bear.

Our mouths meet, not kissing, but simply breathing each other's air, my desire on the verge of madness, the tension so thick, I have to bite my lip to keep from crying out.

And finally, after what feels like an eternity, his hand starts to move.

ELEVEN
ERIN

I've kept my communication with Stefan curt and professional, and so has he. It's Tuesday, and we're meeting for an early dinner after work.

"Erin," Max says. "Can you stay and finish those press releases and the social media plan for the Stella Gallery opening? We need to get them out today."

After securing an internship at this company eight years ago, I moved up to a mid-level position pretty quickly. And then I stalled out. I'm a senior account manager, a position I've been stuck at for five years. It sounds good but pays crap, and if I didn't have a rent-controlled apartment, I'd never be able to stay in the city. I'd like to tell my boss I have plans, but I can't afford to lose my job. And now I have a dilemma.

Do I keep Stefan waiting, or do I try to, diplomatically, explain to Max why I can't stay?

It'll only take me another hour to get out the press releases, and the social media plan can wait until tomorrow. So, I opt for a middle ground, splitting the difference. I tell Max that I can get the press releases out before I leave, and that I'll have the social media plan first thing in the morning. He's just being neurotic. We have plenty of time. Of course, I don't say that to him.

Max is a bit of a gossip and a total opportunist, though, so I add, "I have a date tonight. With a rich guy. Who's some kind of art dealer. He lives in the Hamptons." I smirk.

Almost daily, Max dresses in skinny jeans and an untucked button-down shirt, dark blue or gray, sort of like a uniform, and this day is no exception. Through thick hipster glasses, his eyes widen. "Do tell," he says, slipping into the chair next to my desk, leaning in with an eager look on his face.

I don't have an office. We're sort of in the hallway. It's not a big company.

"I don't want to jinx it," I say. "But if there's anything he can do for the firm, I'll be sure to follow up with you."

"Good girl," he says, and he pats the top of my head.

"Stop it," I say, batting his hand away as he chuckles.

He's trying to be chummy. It's not a sexual thing, but it's still demeaning.

And then I text Stefan, telling him I'm going to be thirty minutes late.

In a few minutes, he responds.

No problem.

Score one for Stefan.

And then a fantasy flashes before my eyes.

A fantasy where I marry Stefan, and I proudly proclaim to Max and the rest of them that I'm leaving this shitty job. And they proceed to kiss my ass, because now I'm *somebody* to them, not merely their little underling, a nobody from Brooklyn—and not even the trendy part.

Everything is relative, I realize now. Before my first trip to the Cosmopolitan Club, I didn't know I was, comparatively speaking, from a low-income family. We had food on the table. A clean, if basic apartment. Friendly neighbors. I enjoyed our summer outings at Coney Island, where I honed my swimming skills. That changed the day my mother took me to an employee appreciation lunch at the club. I must have been around eight years old. I was her date, since my dad was gone by then.

The exterior wasn't much. I'd seen fancier buildings in Manhattan. But when I entered and took in the grand marble staircase, the sparkling crystal chandelier, the elegant, refined décor? My world changed.

I also saw my mother in a different light. It was fine, during the lunch. It was an employee appreciation lunch, after all, and she was a well-liked club receptionist. But as we were walking out, an older woman in a crisp, white suit with her hair in a low bun grabbed my mother by the arm and spun her around.

"Mary!" the woman thundered. Her purple-patterned scarf slipped down, exposing her chicken neck, and she promptly adjusted it. "The table I requested isn't available. I put this reservation in with you personally. This is totally unacceptable. I need you to take care of this immediately."

"I'm sorry, Cynthia. But I'm not working right now. This is my daughter, and we're here for the employee lunch."

She let out a huff. "Fine." This Cynthia woman shot a glance in my direction and rolled her eyes. "I'll get the general manager."

"No, no," my mother said. "I'll see what I can do." Mom turned to me. "Erin, wait here a minute, would you, dear?"

Dear?

"That's... well, thank you, Mary," she said. "But you know how it is. And I want the table I reserved. I mean, how will it look if I'm over in the corner by the service door?"

When my mother left, the woman addressed me. "Your mother is a hard worker. We're lucky to have her," she said, as if that excused her behavior.

It was my mother's tone of voice that got me, not her actions. Mom is a legend in our neighborhood. She once chased a guy who snatched her friend's purse and tackled him, right there on our street. But with this woman, my mother's voice was sickeningly sweet and an octave higher than normal.

When she returned, problem solved, I asked, "Who was that?"

"Oh," Mom said. "She's one of the rich guy's wives." Like that explained everything. "Their biggest problem in life is deciding what to wear, and their biggest coup is getting the best table at a place like this." She shook her head, as if pitying the woman.

I didn't know what a coup was, but from that point on, I knew I wanted to be one of them. I seriously don't know how my mother could stand it, being around the superrich all the time. Kissing up to them. She never envied them, though. Or if she did, she didn't tell me about it. My mother, who also had a side job on the weekends, helping out at a pizza parlor near our house.

I only have vague memories of my father. He was a firefighter and died in the line of duty. Not because of the fire. A beam fell and hit him in the head. He died of a brain hemorrhage when I was three, which explains why I have no siblings. But I do have a large, extended Irish clan, full of cousins and aunts and uncles. Salt of the earth types, with a few tough guys mixed in, the kind who "know people." The kind you don't want to mess with.

Why am I thinking about them now?

I suppose it's because of my fantasy. If I got married, who would walk me down the aisle? A deep, primal longing pummels me in the pit of my stomach, and my eyes start to water. I never feel emotional about my father when I think of him. Normally, I feel detached, like it's something that happened to someone else, or the plot of a book I read. I wonder what's changed.

Max walks by and sees me, and I sniff up the tears.

His eyes narrow on me. "What happened? Did that rat bastard cancel on you?"

"No," I say. "It's... my friend. She got some bad news."

"Well, aren't you the compassionate one?" Max says this with some skepticism in his tone, but leaves it at that. "If you want to do the press releases tomorrow, Erin, it's fine. I'm just being neurotic. We've got time."

"No, I'm almost done," I say. "But thanks."

Maybe Max isn't so bad, after all.

"SORRY I'M LATE," I say. "Last minute request from the boss."

Stefan's seated at the bar, drinking a martini. He's more casual today, wearing a sport jacket over a dark polo shirt and khakis. Surprisingly, I like sporty Stefan. He's even got a little stubble dusting his cheeks, which makes him look a little more rugged, less manicured.

We're at a trendy spot in midtown, full of chrome and glass, with high-end modern art on the walls. A spot he picked, but it's one I like. Again, I'm wondering if he's done some digging around on me.

"I'm just glad you made it," he says. "I've missed you."

He leans over and gives me a steamy kiss.

I try to resist his charms and fail miserably.

But what kind of game is he playing? He must know that most guys are more attentive in the early stages of a relationship. I wonder if it's a tactic, or if that's just his personality.

Out of sight, out of mind.

"I, um, I've missed you, too," I reply.

"You don't sound too sure about that," he says.

I let out a sigh.

The bartender comes over.

"Champagne cocktail?" Stefan asks me.

"Sure," I say. Looking over at the bartender, I add, "Thank you."

"What's wrong?" Stefan's brow furrows, and my gut tells me this isn't a tactic. He seems genuinely puzzled by my standoffishness.

I'm sure that most guys like him are used to women kissing their asses. I mean, he's got it all. Looks. A house in the Hamptons. A driver. A sexy accent. But I'm not built that way. And even if I blow it with him, I owe it to myself to be true to my feelings.

I'm not sure about the timing, though. We're not at a place where I can be demanding. There's no commitment, implied or otherwise. We haven't even talked about being exclusive, an awkward conversation under the best of circumstances.

After a few minutes of uncomfortable silence, I decide to be bold.

"You're sending me mixed messages," I say. "And I don't like it."

Sitting back, I cross my arms.

Stefan's eyes widen. "Mixed messages?"

"You're... hot and cold," I tell him.

Taking a sip of my drink, I let my words linger in the air.

"Hot and cold?" he asks. "How so?"

I go on to recount his crimes against romance. He ghosted me for nearly a week. He left me Saturday night without much explanation. And then I barely heard from him after the first weekend we slept together.

"I don't hop into bed with just anyone, Stefan. I'm not like that," I proclaim.

He flashes me a cheeky grin. "Good to know."

I let out a huff. "If you're not going to take this seriously..."

His look turns earnest, like he's really trying to understand me, and failing miserably. "I'm taking it very seriously, Erin. More than you know."

"What's that supposed to mean?"

"It means I'm not good at this kind of thing." He shrugs. "I'm not good at reading people. If you wanted me to stay Saturday night, why didn't you invite me? It was your home. I didn't want to be... presumptuous. And you can text me, too, you know. It's not the Middle Ages."

This catches me totally by surprise.

Stefan feels insecure about me?

Sorry, I'm not buying it. But it does show me that he

cares about me, if he's willing to make something like that up on the fly. At least he didn't tell me to take a hike.

"Nobody texted in the Middle Ages, Stefan," I say.

He smiles.

I let out a sigh. "Truthfully, I hate this part of relationships. Where everything is so... up in the air. I like clarity."

"Me too," he says. "So, let's go old school."

"What do you mean?"

He takes my hand in his, and for a moment, I'm freaking out.

Is he going to propose or something?

That would be too much.

Way too much.

"Erin Donovan," Stefan says. "Will you be my girlfriend?"

His smile is cautious, as if he's genuinely nervous that I'll turn him down.

A warm smile spreads up my face.

It's the damn sweetest thing that's ever happened to me.

"Stefan Ziegler," I reply. "I would be honored to be your girlfriend."

"To clarity," he says.

We toast.

And I giggle like a schoolgirl for the rest of the night.

TWELVE
ERIN

It's been over twenty years since I set foot in this place. This time, though, things are different. I'm different. Not so easily impressed. The décor strikes me as dated. The food, I notice, is not that great. One step up from banquet fare.

The meal started off okay. An old-school shrimp cocktail. Colossal prawns hooked over a crystal glass filled with crushed ice. Served, of course, with tangy cocktail sauce and a lemon wedge encircled in finely woven cloth to hold back the pits.

But the main dish, some kind of Asian fusion chicken concoction that's trying too hard to be trendy, missed the mark completely. I pick at my rubbery chicken and scrape off the sauce with my fork. It's way too sweet and feels loaded with MSG. My advice is, go with the prime rib or the grilled salmon. Leave the trendy dishes to the pros.

The company, however, is second to none. Ever since Stefan asked me to "go steady," we've been like two love-birds, flitting about town foraging for food, then retreating to our nest to snuggle and... well, you know.

It was his idea to meet at the Cosmopolitan Club for lunch. He's suggested it a few times and I've brushed off the idea. He has a family membership through his father, and he knows my mother worked here, but I haven't told him much more than that.

I'm not sure why he was so insistent on it, but I'm glad I finally capitulated. This class of people had such an outsized impact on me when I was young. But now I can see they are just like everyone else, except maybe a little duller.

Everything seems muted here. The colors. The emotions. The vibe. It makes me realize how vibrant and lively my family is. And now that I'm one of the haves. Now that I'm here as a guest and not the daughter of the servile class, I realize the place is really no big deal.

I imagine that Stefan wanted to take me here to show me that I've arrived. He knows I'm insecure about my humble origins. It's nice that he wants me to feel special. But it isn't having that effect on me. Instead, it's making me realize there's nothing special about this place, or these people.

"How does it feel, being back here?" he asks, between bites of his prime rib. Stefan knows his way around a place like this. No rubber chicken for him.

"It's fine," I say. "I'm just happy to see you in the middle of a workday." This has never happened before.

Stefan bites his lip, as if he's nervous, and I find this so totally endearing. "Should we not have come here? You don't seem to like your meal. Did I screw up again? Is it bothering you, to be back here?"

My heart melts. "No, Stefan. Of course it's not bothering me. It's not like I have PTSD. They didn't tie me up in a basement and hold me for ransom or anything."

He lets out a sigh. "It's just, you told me about your

mother. And how she felt about working here. And how you felt out of place when she took you here those few times. I wanted you to feel like you fit. They were lucky to have your mother. And I'm lucky to have you, here with me."

I try not to take offense at the fact that he's somewhat pitying me and just be happy that he cares enough to take me here—and then feel bad about it.

Resting my hand on his, I smile. "I'm having a nice time. But you know what would make it even nicer?"

"What's that?" he asks.

Flashing him a sexy smile, I say, "Skipping dessert and going back to your place. I took the afternoon off."

"I have a better idea," he says.

Then he asks for the check.

On the way out, our heads turn toward a man a little older than us, making a scene at the front desk, barking something about a reservation that can't be found. The employee, a middle-aged woman, tries to calm him down as the irate patron wags a finger in her face. It's clear that she's frightened. He's closing in on her personal space.

Then the jackass pounds his fist on the desk and his eyes bug out. "What do I need to do to get through to you?"

The woman shrinks back.

Stefan rolls his eyes. "Wait here," he says.

He taps the guy on the shoulder.

The guy whips around, about to pounce.

But then he sees who it is and stops.

His face blanches.

"Oh, I was just—"

Stefan narrows his eyes on him. "This is not behavior becoming of a gentleman. Leave now. And tell your boss he's just lost his biggest client."

"Mr. Zeigler. I can explain." The man's face is red now, but I'm not sure if it's from shame or anger.

Stefan leans in. "I told you. Leave. Now. Is it my accent? Or do you have a hearing problem?"

"Sure." He does as he's told, but as soon as Stefan turns away, I see him shoot daggers back in Stefan's direction.

Stefan rushes over to the woman. "I'm so sorry you had to endure that, Caroline. I assure you, that man won't be bothering you again."

As we head out the door to our surprise destination, I ask, "Who was that guy?"

He rolls his eyes. "Hedge fund new money douchebag. Or should I say, former hedge fund new money douchebag." Then he grins. "His boss will fire him before he lets my account go."

Stefan rarely swears, at least not in English. This makes me giggle. I like tough guy Stefan, although the douchebag is quite a bit bigger than him. I'd watch my back in a dark alley if I were Stefan, but he seems unfazed.

"Come on," he says as he takes me by the hand.

"Where are we going?" I ask.

"You'll see."

NOW THIS IS MORE *like it.*

A suite at The Plaza Hotel.

I feel like Eloise. That was my favorite series as a kid, but I could never afford to stay here. We did high tea a few times, but even that was a budget-killer.

I'm wrapped in Stefan's arms and he's stroking my hair, something he loves to do and can't seem to get enough of. His appetite for me only seems to be growing, and I can't fight the fact that I'm hopelessly falling for him.

Hard.

This could very well end in heartbreak, but I don't think it will. My gut says that his feelings for me are genuine. That he actually loves the real me. Still, he hasn't said it yet. And there's that voice in my head that says proceed with caution.

Or is that Lucy's voice?

Or my mother's?

But then Stefan takes me by the shoulder and guides me around to face him. He looks me in the eye, as if reading my mind, and brushes a stray hair from my face.

"I meant what I said that first weekend, Erin. You're the most real woman I've met in a very long time. And there's nowhere else I'd rather be than here with you. I love being with you. It makes me feel alive."

But does he love me?

It's been a month and a half.

How long is too long to say it?

How long is too soon?

"I love being with you too, Stefan."

And we leave it at that.

Stefan and I have been seeing each other for close to two months now, and we've settled into a pattern. We spend the weekends together when he's not traveling, at his place in the Hamptons, and we share one or two nights in the city together during the week, usually at my place. Stefan seems to prefer it, which I find strange and endearing in equal parts.

His apartment is some sort of corporate rental, devoid of charm or personality, so perhaps that's why. It's large, though, with a nice view of the Chrysler Building, a doorman, and an elevator. I'm in a third-floor walk-up with a view of a brick wall. Maybe he likes the exercise.

My apartment is more intimate than his Hamptons house, so on a few occasions, I was able to use the translation app to listen in on some of Stefan's phone conversations. It's not perfect, but it works pretty well.

And from what I've heard, I'm feeling better about him. Even if he sounds angry, when I translate the German, he's usually saying something mundane, like *do you know when the shipment will arrive?* I'm starting to feel bad about my eavesdropping, and it might be time to stop. To start to trust him and leave my suspicions behind.

It's Sunday, and we're in the Hamptons now. It's busier than it was last month, and that will only increase as time goes on. Stefan left early to play tennis and I got in a morning swim, although I haven't been using the pool as much as I'd imagined; with Tanner living in the cabana, I find it awkward.

I haven't seen the flirty neighbor woman since that first time I was here, and I've been looking out for her. Maybe they were out of town, or they spend time in the city, like Stefan.

What was her name?

Madilyn?

Marilyn?

Madison.

Yes, Madison.

Who wanted to have coffee.

Because we gals need to stick together.

I suppose if I'm going to be a regular in the Hamptons, I'll need someone with connections to ease me into the social scene. Madison has connections, I'm sure, so while Stefan is out, I decide to go over and say hello. It's quicker through the backyard, but that feels a bit snoopy, like I'd be sneaking up on them.

Dressed in running gear and sneakers after my brisk walk, I head out the long driveway and make my way over to their place. Before I can second guess myself, I'm knocking at the front door. The husband answers.

"Yes? May I help you?" he says, like I'm an axe murderer.

I should have gotten her number from Stefan, but I felt like he might have tried to talk me out of it. He didn't seem too fond of her. Now, of course, I'm second-guessing myself.

"Hi," I say. "I'm Erin. I wanted to stop by and say hello to Madison. I'm Stefan's girlfriend. From next door. She said she wanted to have coffee with me."

His brow furrows. "You're supposed to have coffee with my wife this morning? She didn't mention it to me."

"Um, no," I say. "She just, well, the last time I was here, she mentioned we should do it sometime."

"And you thought that time would be..." He looks at his watch. "Nine fifteen on a Sunday morning?"

"Who is it, Jeremy?" I hear Madison call out.

"Erin. From... next door," he says.

"Oh, invite her in!" she replies.

Jeremy shrugs. "Come in." He shakes his head, seemingly perplexed by his wife's enthusiasm. Not angry, though. More like puzzled.

"Hi, Erin! You're just in time. We're having waffles for breakfast. Would you like to join us?"

"Oh, I don't want to intrude. But I didn't have your number, and I haven't seen you around, so I thought I'd come over and we could... make a coffee date."

Madison waves off my concerns. "You're here now. Join us. I'm almost done making breakfast. We've been on an extended vacation. That's why you haven't seen me. Eastern Europe. A heritage trip, of sorts. With the kids."

"That must have been lovely," I say.

"Have a seat." She motions to the island countertop, and I sit on one of the sleek swivel chairs that faces the window, with a stunning view of the bay.

Their house is similar to Stefan's but more homey. Lived-in. Not so pristine. The cabinets are dark cherry, where his are white, which gives off a warmer feel, and there's signs of family life scattered around the living room and kitchen. Sandals and sneakers in various sizes near the front door. Kids' backpacks on the wood floor next to the sofa. A striped blue and white beach towel draped over a wooden lounge chair on the back deck. In the kitchen, a stainless bowl full of batter, some dripping down its side, next to a waffle iron. The scent of browning batter filling the air, making my stomach growl.

"Thanks, if you don't mind. Stefan's off playing tennis. And I feel a little awkward at home with..." I stop myself, because I realize that I'm not sure if it's common knowledge that Tanner, his jailbird brother, is staying there. "Alone, in someone else's house."

She smirks. "With a convicted felon," Madison adds. "Everyone knows about Stefan's brother, but it was nice of you to catch yourself. He's harmless, I promise. Art fraud is hardly a crime. Half the art out there is probably fake. Don't worry, Erin. Tanner's not a threat to you."

This seems a little strange to me, that someone on Madison's social level wouldn't care about a convicted felon living on her street. But maybe there are more rich white-collar criminals than I realize, hiding out in here in the Hamptons.

"So," she says. "What do you do for a living?"

I proceed to tell her, and this raises an eyebrow from her. "Is that how you met Stefan? Through your work?"

"No," I say. "I met him at a bar, believe it or not."

"What a strange coincidence. You're both in the art business, and you met at a bar? That's... curious."

I shrug.

What is she getting at?

Does she think I engineered it?

Is she trying to make trouble?

"And what do *you* do?" I ask her, a slightly snarky tone in my voice.

She probably does nothing, and maybe I shouldn't have asked her that question. But with women like her, you can't be too passive, or they'll eat you alive. Under my friendly exterior, I'm a tough chick from Bay Ridge, and I need to let her know I'm no pushover.

She sighs. "Before I had my children, I was an interior designer."

"It shows," I say. "Your home is lovely."

Madison smiles. "Thanks. But now..." She motions to the waffle iron and bowl of batter sitting on the counter and shrugs. "I've been thinking about getting back into design, at least part-time."

"You should," I say. "If it makes you happy."

Madison's mouth twists and she bites her lower lip, gazing off into space for a bit, as if the very idea of considering her own happiness is a novel one.

A burning smell starts to waft out of the waffle iron.

"Oh crap!" Madison pulls the waffle iron plug out of the wall, flips up the top, and extracts the burning waffle.

A young voice calls out. "Again, Mom?"

I turn and see a little guy, maybe seven or so, with light brown hair in a bowl cut and a half-grown-in front tooth. He's adorable.

She smiles at him, then she says to me, "I can't multitask."

"What's multitask?" the boy asks.

"Do two things at the same time. Talk, and make breakfast."

"Mom, you burn stuff even when nobody's here," he says, shaking his head. "But you're good at other stuff, so don't worry."

With that, he takes off.

"That's my son, Oliver."

"He's precious. And so sweet, the way he tried so hard not to hurt your feelings. You should be proud, raising a son like that."

She smiles. A contented, if somber, smile. "I guess you're right. I wonder what he thinks I'm good at. I'll have to ask him."

"What do you think you're good at?" I ask.

Madison pauses. "I'm good at raising nice people, apparently."

"Well, then, you're doing the world a favor. Still, maybe think about getting back into your career. It's nice to have something you can call your own."

I'm shocked at the words coming out of my mouth.

Wasn't this what I wanted?

A life of luxury, where I didn't have to work?

Why am I telling this lady of leisure to get a job?

WE'RE FINISHING UP BREAKFAST, and I'm glad I came over. Under her steely exterior, Madison seems like a nice person, if a little lonely and unfulfilled. The son is adorable. The daughter is at that awkward age, just before puberty. She's a little chubby, but I bet she'll shoot up and slim down inside of a year.

Still, Madison seems concerned. She tells the daughter not to have a second helping of waffles, and Jeremy shoots her a look. I can't imagine my mother ever saying something like that to me. I come from a family of hearty eaters, and we've never apologized for that.

Suddenly, I've got bigger problems.

A wave of nausea rises up in me.

I struggle to hold it back, hoping they don't notice.

"Excuse me," I say, bolting to the bathroom, thankful that I've been there once this morning, because I don't think I'd have time to ask where it is.

Once inside, I hurl toward the toilet, not in time to lift up the seat or aim.

Some of it goes into the bowl, but much of it lands elsewhere.

This isn't going to be something I can hide from them.

I'm mortified.

What will they think of me?

I know her son implied that she's a bad cook, but this bad?

Bad enough to give us food poisoning?

Are the rest of them sick?

Or is it just me?

And if it is just me, then why?

Did she poison me or something?

Maybe she's not as nice as she seems.

I chuckle at that ludicrous thought.

And then I barf some more.

FOURTEEN
ERIN

"Are you okay?" Madison asks from the bathroom door.

I've been in here a good ten minutes. That, along with the look on my face when I went bolting into the bathroom, probably tells her I'm not, but what else is she supposed to say?

"I'm fine now, but still a little queasy. But your bathroom, not so much."

I open the door a crack and ask if she has any cleaning supplies. Madison tells me she does but assures me that she can take care of it.

"It's my stomach," I say. "I threw up. Maybe I have the flu or something."

"For a minute there, I thought I might have poisoned my whole family." Madison laughs, and I am grateful that she's trying to lighten the mood.

My hands are shaking. I'm so embarrassed. What am I going to tell Stefan?

"I cleaned up as best I could, and washed the floor with

soap and water," I tell her. "But if you hand me some cleaning supplies, I'll do a better job."

"Don't worry about it, Erin. Just come out. It's fine. These things happen. Drink some club soda when you get back to Stefan's place. I'd offer to get you some, but if you do have a stomach flu…" She shrugs.

"I don't know what else it could be. I'm so sorry. I'll go right now. You certainly don't need this ripping through your household."

"Do you have any allergies?" Madison asks.

"Just strawberries," I say.

"No strawberries in the waffles," she says. "Any other flu symptoms? Headache? Body aches?"

I step out of the bathroom, closing the door behind me. "No. Maybe something I ate last night did this to me. Please tell everyone it was nice to meet them. And I'm sorry," I say.

She hands me my purse and ushers me toward the front door.

"You don't need to be sorry, Erin. It's not your fault."

"I feel fine now," I say. "It's so weird."

I'm about halfway out the door when she opens it again. "There's one other possibility," she says. She hesitates, and then she continues. "It happened to me. With Oliver."

My eyes widen, and my stomach drops to the floor. "Are you suggesting…"

She shrugs. "I don't want to pry into your personal life. But it would be an explanation."

"Oh, no, no, no," I assure her. "It's not possible."

"Okay, well, it's not *impossible*, unless you two are not…" She shakes her head. "I'm overstepping here. But if that's the cause, this won't be the last time. I know that from experience. Just something to tuck away. In case it doesn't resolve in a few days."

My head feels as if the blood is draining from it.

Feeling dizzy, I grab the door frame to steady myself.

Madison reaches for me.

"I'm okay," I say.

But I'm not.

Because, come to think of it, I'm late.

I'm on a mini pill, and sometimes that causes me to skip a month.

I thought nothing of it.

Could she be right?

We say our goodbyes, and my panic mushrooms as I walk back over to Stefan's house.

This would be a disaster. Stefan might think I did this on purpose, to trap him. I knew a woman at work who was dating a hedge fund guy worth tens of millions. It wasn't serious, and she claimed she didn't get pregnant on purpose.

But the minute she told him, he hung up on her. The next phone call she got was from his attorney. That's how these guys operate, she told me. Some of them won't even have intercourse with women they're so afraid of getting scammed by the baby trap.

Then there's the fact that I'm not sure if Stefan is a criminal, or that it's in my best interest to stay with him. One thing is for sure. I need to keep this quiet. From him. From Madison. Until I know more.

I was looking forward to a nice, quiet weekend in the country, but now I just want to get home. Where I can get a home pregnancy test and find out for sure that I'm absolutely, one hundred percent, not pregnant with Stefan's baby. We were planning to go back to the city early Monday morning. I could make a case for heading back this afternoon, but it would raise a red flag if we spent the night in different apartments. I think I'm stuck with him until Monday.

In the meantime, my best-case scenario is that I find Stefan puking his guts out when I get home. I'm going to have to tell him what happened at Madison's. If he's not sick, I'll blame it on what I ate last night. We went out, thankfully. He had steak. I had shrimp, but we shared a clam appetizer. And I'll use that as an excuse not to drink tonight.

I can do this, I tell myself.

Scenarios play out in my head, if the unthinkable comes to be. If I have his baby, I realize, I'll be tethered to Stefan, whether I want to be or not. Maybe I could move to Florida with my mother? But only if I don't tell him and just leave. Is that even legal? Rich people have expectations. If I have a baby with him, my life will never be my own again, even if we don't end up together.

Suddenly, I find myself very protective of my independence.

What is wrong with me?

Isn't this what I've wanted all my life?

No, it's not.

Not like this.

It can't happen like this.

Can it?

FIFTEEN
MADISON

The first thing I do, even before cleaning the bathroom, is grab my burner from my purse and head up to my bedroom to alert Tanner to this new development. Another potential heir to the Ziegler fortune could really screw things up for him.

But Jeremy won't leave me alone.

He follows me up to the bedroom.

Who is that woman?

Why did you invite her in?

What if she has Ebola?

My husband has a good sense of humor, I'll give him that.

I managed to tuck the phone into the waistband of my yoga pants just before he came into our bedroom. Thankfully, I'm not wearing a crop top, but my tank top rides up, so I'm sticking out my stomach and pulling the shirt down with my right hand, hoping he doesn't notice the slight bulge.

"It's fine," I say. "She had seafood last night. It's probably food poisoning. Let me go disinfect the bathroom, just in case. You keep the kids out of range."

But he won't leave it alone.

"Why did you invite her to eat breakfast with us? That's our family time," he says.

Jeremy is suspicious, I know this.

So, I go on the offensive.

"Oh my God, Jeremy. I'm trying to be a nice neighbor. Is that so hard to believe?"

I push past him, shaking my head, and go on my way.

Where are the cleaning supplies?

I haven't cleaned my own bathroom in decades.

Do we even have cleaning supplies?

I find some rubber gloves, a sponge, Ajax, and 409 in the hall closet and lock myself in the guest bathroom. Before I put on the gloves, I fire off a text to Tanner, telling him we need to talk. I stop short of explaining myself.

Something holds me back. Maybe it's the steely look he got in his eyes when he talked about Stefan and the inheritance. He can be a bit of a hothead. On second thought, maybe I should keep this from him until I know more.

So, I don my gloves and start cleaning.

It surprises me that I don't mind it so much. I zone out, focusing on the tile and the grout and the porcelain; in the moment for a change, not ruminating or second-guessing or regretting.

That's what yoga is supposed to do for me, put me into a state of mindfulness. But it doesn't. Usually, my mind is racing for the entire hour—about the kids, Jeremy, Tanner, my life—even when I'm stretched out on the floor in Savasana, when everyone else seems to almost fall asleep.

After twenty minutes or so locked in here with the

fumes, I decide it's time to face the family. I don't plan to make a habit of this. Jeremy is not going to stop, so I'll need to give him a better explanation.

The kids are up in their rooms, having some quiet time. We're planning to go to the beach on the south shore in about an hour to meet some other families.

"So," he says, his brow furrowed, his upturned palm hovering between us. "What just happened here? Why did you invite her in?"

I notice he's cleaned up the breakfast dishes, and I thank him for that. My husband knows me. Very well. And I know him. It's not easy to fake it, so I give him something real.

I let out a sigh. "She's different from the other women I know around here."

"Different, how?"

"She's one of those... struggling career girls, living in the city."

This is a partial truth. She intrigues me, although I would rather she didn't come by with Jeremy here, for a number of reasons.

"So she's your charity case?" he asks.

I roll my eyes. "No, Jeremy. I mean, she's self-made. Like you." I throw him a bone, because Jeremy loves to think of himself that way when, in reality, he had every advantage in life. "She's... interesting. And she got me thinking."

"Thinking about what?" he asks.

"About my career. And that I miss it. Maybe I'd like to start designing again."

My husband shrugs. "Do what you want, Madison," he says. "But you know how my job is these days, and it's just getting worse. I need to watch my back, with all the up-and-comers vying for my spot. So, remember, my job comes first. But I understand if you're bored and you need a hobby."

Just when I thought I didn't completely despise him.

I could strike back.

Tell him my career is not a hobby.

Remind him that my inheritance paid for the down payment on this place, a home he never would have been able to afford by the time he made enough money to live in Southampton, since property values have more than doubled since we bought this place.

But all the money is commingled now; all my premarital assets. So, I don't protest.

Instead, I picture Tanner's rock-hard abs.

I think about the feel of his hands on my body.

The way he grabs me. Devours me.

I look my husband up and down, and I respond: "Speaking of hobbies, you need to get back to the gym, Jeremy. Spruce up your look. Ageism is real, even for men, and you're starting to look a little past your prime. Our lifestyle is expensive. And so are my hobbies. So yeah, watch your back with the up-and-comers. And you might want to watch your front, too."

There's a hurt look in his eyes, because he knows I'm right.

And it almost makes me feel bad.

Almost.

But he started it.

He was the first to betray our marriage vows.

So, if my heart has hardened, that's on him.

SIXTEEN
ERIN

I was able to get through the weekend without revealing much of anything. I told Stefan about the incident at Madison's house, and I threw suspicion on the seafood from the night before. We decided to go back to the city Sunday afternoon, and I used my upset stomach as an excuse to sleep alone in my apartment.

I'd like to say I ran out and got a home pregnancy test and faced this head-on, but I couldn't bring myself to do that after he left. I gave it one more night, to see how I'd feel in the morning. I was fine until I drank coffee this morning, and then I started to feel queasy again. I didn't throw up, mainly because there wasn't much in my stomach. So, before work, I picked up a few tests, because I know in the early days they can be unreliable. Better to check and double-check.

And then I left them sitting in my apartment. I couldn't face this alone, so I called Lucy and she agreed to meet me after work. I'm headed home now.

Max sensed that something was wrong today. I finished up what I'd been working on. And then he gave me another assignment. A new gallery in Noho that's bought out an old exercise facility and wants to transform it into a modern art gallery.

I thought of Madison.

"Do they need an interior designer?" I asked.

He shrugged. "No idea. I could ask."

For some reason, I shared with him my breakfast fiasco, and that I'd left most of it in the Bradford's guest bathroom. I told him the interior design lead might be a way to salvage the relationship and gain back my dignity. I also pointed out that Madison is old money wealthy, something Stefan told me on Sunday, and Max's eyes lit up.

"Well done, Erin. You're a real team player."

Later, when I was looking up information on morning sickness and pregnancy and the minipill, Max walked by, and I slammed my laptop shut.

But maybe not in time.

"What're you, a spy or something?" he asked.

"If I am, I'm a pretty lousy one." I offered him a nervous smile.

"You've earned your keep for the day, Erin. If you're doing some online shopping or whatever, it's fine with me. I'm not a micromanager."

"Thanks, Max," I said.

Then he winked at me and went on his way.

<hr>

"JUST GO in and pee on the damn thing already!" Lucy's standing with one hand on her hip and the pee stick in the other one, holding it out for me to grab.

I've been procrastinating for over an hour.

"Okay, I can do this," I say.

Grabbing the stick, I head into the bathroom and do my thing, then I come out and we pace around the room for a few minutes.

"I can't look," I say.

Time is more than up, but I'm being a wimp.

I go through all of my fears again.

Stefan will think it's a trap.

What if Stefan is a criminal?

I'm not ready to be a mother.

The thought of a person popping out from between my legs terrifies me.

"I can't know before you do," Lucy says. "You have to be the one to look. And whatever it is, you can handle it. We can handle it. You're not alone, I promise. Whatever you decide, I'm in it with you. A hundred percent."

She hugs me, and it feels nice. Under her kick-ass exterior, she's a great friend. And I couldn't have a better person in my corner.

So, I march into the bathroom to face my future.

Looking at the stick, my stomach sinks, and I'm not prepared for the wave of emotion that overcomes me.

I come out of the bathroom with tears pooling in my eyes.

"I can't believe it," Lucy says. She wipes away the tear that escaped and ran down my face. "You're pregnant, Erin. You're not dying. Don't worry. It will be great."

I shake my head. "No," I say. "I'm not pregnant. It's negative."

LUCY STAYED AND CONSOLED ME. We opened a bottle of wine to celebrate, but it made my stomach sick so I dumped mine out. I guess I do have some kind of food poisoning, or a bug.

It's a strange feeling, to not know my own mind.

I was sure this was what I wanted.

To be not pregnant.

So why do I feel sad?

Is this normal?

Last night before she took off, Lucy reminded me that it's pretty early in the game, and that at-home pregnancy tests are more sensitive in the morning. She's right, of course, which is why I bought more than one.

So, I did another test this morning, and I'm waiting to check the results. I drank coffee without incident, though, so I'm thinking the one last night was right. My stomach seems fine now. It was probably bad shrimp. Still, it's better to know for sure.

Without Lucy here, I feel very alone. But not in the sense of fearing single motherhood, all alone in the big, bad world kind of alone. No, I feel incomplete, like I'm missing something I didn't know I even wanted—and I probably never had to begin with. It makes no sense.

But I square my shoulders, pick up the stick, and look.

My eyes widen, and once again, tears pool in my eyes.

Happy ones, this time, with a touch of panic mixed in.

The test says I'm pregnant.

Now what?

It's been two weeks and I still haven't told Stefan. Luckily, he went out of town for a week, and I used that time to visit my OB and confirm my at-home findings. Yep. No mistake there. I'm basically, totally, and completely... seven weeks pregnant.

The morning sickness is on and off. Tonight, I'm planning to tell him, and my stomach is in knots, but not because of the pregnancy. I haven't even told my mother yet. In fact, Lucy is the only one who knows, aside from my doctor who suggested that, since I'm not past the first trimester danger zone, I could wait a little longer to tell people, to make sure it sticks. I thought about waiting to tell Stefan, before I upend my life, until I'm past that point.

But then I decided it wasn't fair to him. I got confirmation last week from my OB, and he deserves to know. The more I put it off, the worse it will be. It's Friday night and we're at my apartment. I told him I needed to work late, and that I preferred to go to the Hamptons in the morning. He wanted to go out to eat, but I asked if we could stay in. I don't want to have this conversation in front of strangers, or with his brother lurking in the shadows.

Rather than cook, I picked up some Italian food on my way home. Cheese ravioli and salad. Bland and basic. I still can't look at shellfish after what happened two weeks ago. Stefan brought a bottle of Chianti, and not the cheap kind.

"Ready?" he says.

Then he pops out the cork and pours two glasses for us. I should stop him, but I don't. Instead, I let him set them on my dining table and I serve our meals.

We sit, and he toasts.

"To us," he says.

But rather than lift it to my lips, I rest my glass on the table.

"You're mad at me again," he says, shaking his head. "I'm sorry. I should have contacted you more often. I got busy."

Come to think of it, he didn't text or call me all that much, and it's funny that something that was a big deal to me a few weeks ago seems pretty trivial now that I've got more pressing concerns.

"No," I say. "It's not that. But I have to tell you something."

I take his hands, but I can't bring myself to speak.

"What is it, Erin? You're worrying me. Is it us?"

"No," I say. "It's about me."

His eyes widen. "Are you sick?" he asks. "Is this about what happened at Madison's house?"

"Sort of, yeah." I pause. "But I'm only sick... in the morning."

I offer a hesitant shrug.

Then my head tilts to the side, waiting for things to click.

Maybe it's a language thing, because he looks more confused than before.

And then it hits him.

His jaw drops. "Wait. Erin. Are you telling me..."

Stefan's mouth hangs open, and he stops mid-sentence.

My face flushes, and I struggle to breathe.

Because he's not smiling.

He's not talking.

He's just sitting there, staring at me, like he wants to say something, but he can't.

So, I continue. "You can be as involved as you want. I expect nothing from you, Stefan. But I thought I should let you know."

He narrows his eyes at me. "What?" he says. "Are you suggesting—"

"I'm suggesting nothing," I say. "I'm informing you, that's all."

Now his look turns stern, which was not at all what I wanted. "I can be as involved as I want?" he says. "Are you telling me that you are pregnant with my child and you plan to raise this baby by yourself?"

My hands tremble and my lip starts to quiver.

And then the deluge breaks.

I sob, and I'm barely able to catch my breath.

Between the gasps, I manage to get out what I want to say:

"I didn't want it to happen like this. And now you're upset with me. I'm sorry, Stefan. I didn't plan this."

He comes over and hugs me close.

We stay like that for a good long time.

Then he leans back and brushes the hair back from my face. "I'm not upset, Erin. Shocked, maybe. But not upset.

I'm going to be a father. This is, well, this is, officially, the best day of my life. And I'm all in, if you want me to be."

And now he smiles, an ear-to-ear grin.

"Really?" I ask. "But it's so soon for us. We're just getting to know each other."

"We've got nine months. We better move fast."

"Seven months, Stefan. Give or take. It takes a while for things to... percolate." I shrug.

"Right. Wow." He shakes his head. "Well, we better start planning the wedding."

And now it's my turn to look shocked.

"Wedding? What wedding?" I reply.

"My firstborn child is not going to enter this world as a bastard. Of course, we'll be married. As soon as possible. My family will insist."

And then I start to cry again. I'm afraid all this emotion is going to hurt the baby, so I make an effort to get a grip. The father of my child seems totally puzzled by my reaction, and that makes me want to scream.

"What's going on with you?" he asks.

Could he possibly be this clueless?

"Stefan! What kind of proposal is that? It's so presumptuous. I've had more romantic exchanges with my accountant. You're supposed to ask me, not tell me. And we should be in love. Shouldn't we?"

He lets out a breath. "Aren't we, though? In love? I am. I thought you were, too."

"You never said it to me."

"I'm saying it now," he offers. "I love you."

"Only because I'm carrying your child."

"No. That's not true. I swear, Erin. When I saw you sitting in the bar that night, I just knew. It was like being struck by a lightning bolt. I never believed in that before, until you came along. But if you don't feel the same, perhaps I've misread this whole situation."

I sigh.

It sounds good, but how do I know it's the truth?

"I don't want to spend my whole life thinking you're only with me because of an accident," I say.

Stefan rests his head on mine and looks deep into my eyes. I can see little flecks of gold in his. "Then don't think of it as an accident," he says.

"Well, what should I think of it as?"

A warm smile spreads up his face.

"Think of it as fate."

THE ENGAGEMENT

EIGHTEEN
ERIN

"Meet me for lunch, at the sandwich shop on forty-fifth and Lex," Lucy said on the phone this morning, about an hour after I got to work. "We need to catch up. Did you tell Stefan?"

I told her I did, but I plan to surprise her with my news, so I didn't let on about how it went. The day after I told Stefan, before we went to the Hamptons, he came back to my apartment with a ring. A family heirloom with a diamond bigger than I've ever seen in my life, but in a classic setting so it manages to present as tasteful, not garish. That was accompanied by a bouquet of tropical flowers.

He proposed, officially, but he didn't get down on his knee.

I said yes.

It was short and sweet, just like our courtship.

And I finally told my mother. As I expected, she's a little concerned about the timing, but she's over the moon about the idea of being a grandmother. So much so, that she only briefly mentioned that I need to have an attorney look over the prenup, even though Stefan hasn't said anything yet about making me sign one. I'm sure he will, though. I'm not delusional. It would be weirder if he didn't, and his family will probably insist.

Lucy's sitting at a booth when I arrive. I go up to the counter and order, grab a bottle of water, and then I take a seat.

She opens her mouth to speak, but then she sees my hand.

Her eyes widen. "Erin? Are you and Stefan…"

My face breaks into a Cheshire cat grin. I've been holding it back, but now I feel the full weight of the excitement, and I let it wash over me.

"Engaged? Yes! We're getting married in two months. I want you to be my maid of honor."

We chat for a bit as I fill her in on the details, and then she stops to take a call. Spotting my sandwich on the counter, I leave her to go grab it.

Upon return, I study the look on her face.

She doesn't seem to be sharing in my joy.

"What is it?" I ask. "You think it's too soon?"

She lets out a sigh. "A little, but that's not all. There's a reason I wanted to see you in person. And I know this is pretty much the worst time to tell you something like this. But Justin shared this with me last night."

Lucy holds out her phone. It's a photo of a man I've never seen before. He looks to be in his mid-fifties. Salt and pepper hair and a neatly trimmed beard, wearing a suit. Clean cut, with small beady eyes, almost as black as his pupils. He's not unattractive, but the look on his face is terrifying. If looks could kill…

"Am I supposed to know who he is?"

She shakes her head no. "His name is Dimitri Petrov. He's suspected of all kinds of international crimes. Money laundering. Theft and sale of looted art and sculpture."

"Why are you telling me this?" I take a bite of my sandwich, still not catching her drift.

"Because Stefan's had two meetings with him over the last few months. We thought you should know. And Justin's offer still stands. If you want to—"

I stop chewing, and say through a full mouth of food, "Oh my God, Lucy! I can't believe you. You can't let me have this moment, can you?" Then I proceed to choke down my mouthful of roast beef sandwich, my appetite vanishing as my blood starts to boil.

"What are you talking about?" she asks. "I'm trying to protect you."

Lucy won't understand my reaction. I barely understand it myself, so I switch gears. "You said he's... suspected of crimes. Not convicted of them. So what? Half the art pieces in circulation are probably forgeries. Is Stefan the only person in New York City who took a meeting with this guy?"

"I doubt it," she admits.

I roll my eyes and let out a sigh of exasperation. "Why can't you just be happy for me for once?"

Lucy looks hurt, confused. "I don't understand what's happening here. You wanted me to look into him, Erin. Where is all this coming from?"

"I can't do this right now," I say.

Because the truth is, I don't know where it's coming from, but it's coming, and I can't seem to stop it.

So, I abandon my lunch and leave her sitting there, along with my half-eaten sandwich.

ON MY WAY back to work after I stormed out, I grabbed a pizza slice, because although I wasn't very hungry, I knew I needed to eat. It wasn't the healthiest lunch on the planet, but it was better than nothing. For dinner, I'm having roasted chicken, broccoli, and potatoes. Plain food works best for me these days.

Max came by in the afternoon and mentioned that the Noho gallery owner is actually looking for a designer. I'd totally forgotten that I'd mentioned Madison to him. Work doesn't know about the baby or our engagement. I take off the ring when I'm there. I don't need them putting me out to pasture just yet.

This is actually good timing. Madison is pretty connected in terms of the happenings in the Hamptons, so if something is hinky with Stefan and his business and this Dimitri guy, she's sure to have an inkling. A potential client gives me a reason to text her and plan a girls' lunch for this coming weekend.

I'm about done with my meal when I hear my door buzzer.

Maybe it's Stefan, but I hope not. I'm not in the mood to see him. After cooling off, I did some research on Dimitri Petrov. There's not much, but then why would there be? It's not like Wikipedia would have a dossier about his suspected criminal escapades. He seems to be some kind of oligarch, and he's insinuated himself into the social scene in the Hamptons. He divides his time between St. Petersburg and New York.

"It's me," Lucy says. "Can I come up?"

I need to apologize, so although I'm not in the mood for company, I buzz her in.

Greeting her at the door, I get it out of the way. "Sorry I got so upset. I know you're just looking out for me."

Still, my heart's not in it, and I don't know why. Maybe if she hadn't asked me to spy on Stefan again, her warning would have landed better.

I offer her a drink, but she declines. Instead, she guides me to the living room and we sit next to each other on the sofa.

"What did you mean, why can't I be happy for you, for once?" she says.

This conversation has been a long time coming, but it needs to happen. And for once, I open up to her about all of it. The blind spot she has about how her family's money insulates her from the harsh realities of life for people like me. The insecurities I felt growing up. The impostor syndrome I've felt my whole life, attending schools I never could afford, trying to fit myself into a class above my station, and that of my mother's.

"I never thought of you like that, Erin. And I don't think most people did. Most people probably didn't even know."

I know what she means. Working-class people like me from Irish American neighborhoods don't often apply to schools like the one we attended. Parochial schools, sure. But not waspy prep schools. And usually not on financial aid. So yeah, maybe most people there thought I was one of them. My whole family thought it was odd that I applied. They teased me about it. But that's what I wanted, so why am I complaining?

"It's not just that, Lucy. It's that sometimes you can be a little... tone-deaf about my reality."

I go on to explain to her what I've held back for years, for fear of sounding petty or envious. "You say I don't need a man to live large, but you have a man. Your father."

I point out that her parents paid for law school.

Helped her buy a luxury condo.

"You're right," she says. "And I'm sorry that I couldn't see how my words were hurting you. But I didn't mean it like that. I only said things like that because I care about you. And I'm worried that this is all moving too fast, and I don't want a man to have so much power over you."

"It is moving fast," I tell her. "But it's what I want right now. Can you just try and be supportive? That's what I need from you right now. And I certainly don't need you and Justin pressuring me to spy on the father of my child. He's not just some guy I'm dating anymore. So please, support me."

"Yes, Erin. I can do that, if it's what you want. But keep that phone number that Justin gave you handy. Remember Petrov's face. And if you see him around, pay attention, okay? Keep your guard up. Not for Justin and his case, but for your own safety. Maybe it's nothing, but we still have a few months to figure it out. And I promise, if it doesn't work out with Stefan, I've got you."

We hug, and we stay like that for a good long moment.

Now I feel ashamed of myself for the way I've let petty jealousy get the better of me. Lucy's right. I need to look out for myself and my baby. I don't know Stefan that well. His brother is a convicted felon. And compared to most people on the planet, I lead a pretty charmed life. It could always be worse.

"I'm sorry I took it out on you," I say.

"What are best friends for?" she says.

She's never called me that before.

"So, you'll be my maid of honor?" I ask.

"Of course," she says. "And your bodyguard. If anyone tries to fuck with you, they'll need to go through me first."

"You're a force, Lucy Chang."

"So are you, Erin Donovan. And don't you forget it."

"They're engaged?"

Tanner nods. "Yeah," he says. "They're getting married in two months."

He's whipping us up some cappuccinos in the fancy coffee maker. Stefan and Erin won't be here until midday, Tanner assured me, so we're hanging out in the main house, although I'm not sure that's a great idea.

"She must be pregnant," I say. "Why else would he rush this? He didn't say anything about a baby?"

"No, I already told you. Why do you keep asking me the same questions, over and over? It's annoying."

Speaking of annoying, Tanner is grating on my nerves even more than usual today. I'm not sure why. Maybe it's the whiney tone, which is definitely not a turn-on. But I need to manage this relationship very carefully.

"What would that mean for your situation?" I ask this with some trepidation, because I don't want it to seem like I have designs on his inheritance. I've pretty much abandoned the idea of throwing in with Tanner. All he has to show for his efforts is a felony conviction. But I have my reasons for keeping this affair going, at least for a little while longer.

"If Stefan produces an heir, he gets more money, according to the trust. I'm not sure how it would affect the inheritance. But it doesn't matter, because I have a better plan," he says.

"What's that?"

"I'm going to get Stefan arrested. For something big." Tanner flashes me a sly smile. Sensing the shift in mood, he pulls me in and tickles me in my favorite spot. "And I like to share. Stick with me, babe. It'll all work out. I promise."

"Wait. Are you telling me that Stefan is doing something illegal?" I ask.

This kills the vibe. Tanner steps back from me and his expression hardens. "You need to stop asking questions, Madison. Curiosity killed the cat. Remember?"

I need to tread carefully, so I try to move us back in the right direction.

Rubbing up against him, I let out a purring sound.

"That's a good little kitty," he says.

Our mouths meet, and he slides his hand up my inner thigh.

"Let's go back to your place," I say.

"No." He takes me by the hand and leads me to the sofa. "Let's mark our turf," he says, his voice low and sexy. "All of this will be mine, soon enough."

And with that, we fall onto the sofa and melt into one.

IT'S SATURDAY AFTERNOON, and I talked Jeremy into taking the kids to the beach without me, complaining of a headache. I'm in my walk-in closet, even though nobody's home. It's a habit. The kids are out of school now, so I'm parenting more than usual, and it's nice to have some alone time.

I pull out my burner phone and send a text, but not to Tanner.

> Got something for you.

Tucking the burner back into its hiding place, my cell buzzes with a text from Erin, telling me she has a lead for me on a design job.

Wow, what timing.

It would be a lot better to take on something like this when the kids are in school. But I text her back and ask her to come over, because the thought of going back to work sends a zap of energy through me that's even bigger than the charge I got when I started my affair with Tanner.

Plus, I'd love nothing more than to rub that hobby statement in Jeremy's face. I made good money when I worked, and that comment was totally insensitive—not to mention inaccurate. I tell her I can meet in an hour, and she confirms. Maybe I'll get more intel on Stefan and kill two birds with one stone.

Soon, I'm greeting Erin at the door, pretending to know nothing about the engagement. Keeping my baby suspicions to myself. I offer her a mimosa, but she declines.

"Coffee?" I ask.

Erin shakes her head. "Maybe just some club soda," she replies.

"Still fighting that stomach bug?" I ask.

She offers me an apologetic look. "I'm so sorry about that. No, I'm fine. But thanks for asking."

"I need a coffee," I say, and I pop in a k-cup. "Have a seat, Erin."

I saw the giant rock on her finger, but so far, I haven't commented on it. The same one he gave to Amelia. I'm surprised she gave it back. She seemed the type to take him for everything she could get. I wonder if Erin knows she's got a recycled ring on her finger.

As I pop a few ice cubes in a glass and pour some sparkling water into it, I'm trying not to look at her hand.

"Lemon?" I ask, realizing I'll have to try and feign surprise about the engagement. I'll do it when I hand her the glass.

"Sure," she says.

Grabbing one from the veggie bin, I cut off a slice and drop it into her glass.

Handing her the drink, I widen my eyes. "Oh wow! Are you and Stefan...?"

Erin offers me a smile, but it's a half-hearted one. Her lips are pressed, and it seems as if she's forcing it. "Yes. I know, I can hardly believe it myself," she says.

She already knows that I suspect something about a pregnancy, but I can't bring it up. "Well, when it's right, it's right," I say.

"I guess."

Lifting my coffee mug, I say, "To you and Stefan."

We toast.

"Thank you."

"Have you set a date?" I ask.

"Not exactly," she says.

I happen to know it's in two months, but that doesn't mean she's lying. Maybe they haven't set an actual date yet.

"Well, there's no rush, right?" This time, I hold her gaze until she changes the subject.

After a moment, she says, "So, about the job."

"Right. That's why we're here."

Erin tells me about it. A new gallery in Noho. It sounds perfect for me, and I really am grateful for this. She gives me the details, and the woman's name.

"There are no guarantees," she says. "You'll have to compete for it."

"Of course. Thanks for thinking of me. If there's anything I can do for you, just let me know."

"Actually, there is one thing. Did you know Stefan's last girlfriend? Amelia something or other? The one you mentioned when we first met?" I ask.

The woman whose ring is on your finger?

"Amelia Summers? Yes," I say. "But you mean his last fiancé, no?"

Erin's eyes widen, but she catches herself. "Sure," she says. "That's what I meant."

She most certainly did not know.

"Not well," I say. "But yes, I met her a few times. You two look alike from a distance, but not so much up close."

"Do you know why they broke up?"

"Isn't this something you should ask Stefan?"

She lets out a sigh. "He doesn't like to talk about that."

"Tanner said something about the prenup," I blurt out, without thinking.

And then my stomach tenses.

Why did I mention Tanner?

Why would I be talking to Tanner?

It's not lost on Erin. "I didn't realize that you and Tanner—"

Jeremy and the kids come bursting through the door, saving me from having to explain myself, although whatever she's thinking, it's probably not good.

Why are they home so early?

This annoys me. I didn't want Erin to cross paths with my husband.

Then I hear Oliver whimpering, and I rush up to him.

"Jellyfish sting," Jeremy says.

"Oh, honey. Let me get some vinegar," I say to Oliver.

"I'll get out of your hair," Erin says.

Jeremy is cordial to Erin, but I can tell he doesn't like this. I said I had a headache, and I'm sitting with a relative stranger at our kitchen counter. I feel like a horrible mother, so I tend to my son as Erin scurries out of our house.

Abby asks if she should help.

"No, honey, it's fine," I tell her. "Go shower off. I've got this."

"I need to unload the car," Jeremy says.

I tend to my son's jellyfish sting and wipe the tears from his eyes.

"It's getting better, Mommy," Oliver says.

My heart melts. He hasn't called me mommy in over a year. What am I doing, sneaking around with Tanner and neglecting my kids? This isn't me. I need to find a better way of channeling my anger at Jeremy. One that doesn't affect Abby and Oliver.

After I get my son's jellyfish sting under control and send him up to shower, Jeremy comes through the back entrance and into the kitchen.

"What the fuck is going on, Madison?" he says.

"What do you mean?"

"I thought you had a headache."

I let out a sigh. "I did. But Erin has a lead for me on a design job in the city, and—"

"Jesus Christ Madison! Will you get your head out of the clouds?" My husband throws up his hands and storms out.

Gritting my teeth, I fight the wave of emotion welling up inside me. It's not anger, though, which surprises me, because I didn't think my husband could hurt me anymore.

I was wrong.

TWENTY
ERIN

Dimitri Petrov turned out to be a very cordial man, at least on the surface. I couldn't believe it when Stefan and I ran into him while we were seated in the bar area, waiting for our dinner table yesterday evening. I had to fight not to give myself away.

"Stefan," a man behind us said, as he took the seat next to my future husband.

Immediately, I recognized him, even with a smile on his face, which made him look more pleasant. But I didn't let Dimitri's gregarious exterior fool me, because the photo Lucy showed me is forever etched in my mind.

He patted Stefan on the back.

Stefan bristled, but forced a smile.

"Dimitri," Stefan said, leaning back a little from Petrov. "This is my fiancé, Erin Donovan."

"Nice to meet you," I said, waving at him.

Stefan was seated between us, and I was happy about this. I didn't want him to kiss my hand or my cheek or whatever it is Russians do.

"Lovely to meet you, Miss Donovan," he said. "But I think we've met before, no?"

"Please," I said. "Call me Erin. And no, I don't think we have."

Dimitri ordered a shot of Beluga, a top-shelf Russian vodka. We made small talk for a few minutes, but he didn't ask anything more about our engagement or our wedding. Then he asked me what I did.

"I work in art marketing," I said. "For a small firm."

"Interesting. Do you have a card? I dabble. We should keep in touch."

"Sure."

Stefan flinched, ever so slightly.

Handing him a card, I added, "I'm a senior account manager, not one of the principals."

"Well, things can change," Petrov said.

And then he addressed Stefan. "This is a good look on you, my friend. You always struck me as a family man."

Stefan shrugged. "To each his own."

Dimitri let out a hearty laugh.

A stunning brunette with the body and gait of a super-model joined him at the bar, wearing a tight black dress that sat just above the knee. She looked about half his age.

But she didn't sit. "I'm hungry," she said in a breathy tone, placing a hand on Dimitri's shoulder, as if she was on the brink of starvation and needed to steady herself. This wouldn't have surprised me. She was rail thin, with protruding clavicle bones that she wore like a badge of honor, accented with a diamond pendant.

Dimitri downed his shot, and they left for their table.

"What did he mean, that he thought he met me before?" I asked.

"He's probably confused. I don't know him that well."

But my mind flashed again to that ex of his. The one who looks like me. I'm sure that's who he met. I didn't want to spoil the evening, so I let it go.

I wanted to ask Stefan about Dimitri Petrov, but the hostess came over to escort us to our table, and Stefan immediately launched into a discussion of our wedding plans. We'd been at odds over the size and tone of the wedding. I want something small. Stefan wants to invite the town.

"Fifty people," I said. "Tops. Family and close friends."

"It's not that simple," he said. "I have obligations. It's how business is done, Erin. If we have one guest, I need to invite at least a hundred, or people will be offended."

"Well, what if we offend nobody?" I offered.

His brow furrowed. "What are you suggesting?"

"We elope, and then throw a party when we get back. It's a lot less pressure."

Stefan's head tilted to the side. "That's not a bad idea."

And so, we never did get around to discussing Dimitri Petrov, so that's first on my agenda for this morning. I'm not a great liar, so I've decided I'm going to come clean with my future husband about my doubts and clear the air. Running into Petrov last night gives me the perfect opportunity, especially since he asked for my card. I can't start out a marriage with something like this hanging over my head. But I have to pick my moment.

Heading into the kitchen, I stop when I hear Tanner and Stefan, obviously at odds about something.

Stefan's tone is hushed but harsh. "So, that's just a coincidence? That we ran into him?"

"What are you getting at, Stefan?" Tanner says. "I had

no idea where you were going last night. You're getting paranoid."

"You could use a little paranoia," Stefan says. "I'm not the one in an ankle monitor."

"This is bullshit," Tanner says.

And he storms off.

Is he talking about Dimitri Petrov?

Was it not a coincidence that we ran into him last night?

And if so, what does that mean?

"Hey," I say.

I make myself a decaf cappuccino while I search for a way to bring up what I want to talk about. Turns out, I don't get a chance, because Stefan throws me a curveball.

"Erin. I think you should quit your job," he says.

"What? Why?"

"You'll be busy with the baby. And all of our social events. And I'd like to take you both with me when I travel to Europe. You know I have to spend a lot of time there."

"Does this have anything to do with Dimitri Petrov? And that he asked for my card?"

Stefan lets out a sigh. "Not entirely. But yes. You don't want to do business with him, Erin. Trust me on this."

"I'm not stupid, Stefan. I've been in the art business for a while now. I know about the money laundering cases. The forgeries. I'm not that naïve."

"I didn't say you were. But things will be different now. There's a lot at stake. And with families like mine, certain precautions need to be taken. There are dangers. It comes with the territory."

"I'm going to need some clarification on this, Stefan. Exactly what kind of danger am I in? Are you doing something illegal?"

Stefan's eyes widen. "What? No. Why would you even ask me that?"

"I know who Dimitri Petrov is. And you two seem pretty friendly. Then there's your brother. And the fact that you don't tell me much about your business dealings."

Stefan purses his lips. "There are some things I just can't share. My father insists on that. Our family business is complex. Mostly, we deal in natural gas. Petrov has some interest in it. All legitimate. But we own other businesses. And we do some art deals, but not contemporary art. Mostly old masters. My family is well-connected, and thankfully, some buyers still have taste. We work with them. Does that make you feel any better?"

Most of the money laundering is in abstract art. Modern. Contemporary. Not old master works. I know this, and he probably knows that I know this.

Still, he's going to be the father of my child.

I need to trust him, don't I?

"Sure," I say, knowing that I'll meet his father soon enough, so I can judge for myself.

We're headed to Europe, to meet his family and take care of the business side of this marriage. Then we're eloping, to the South of France, but we're not telling anyone until after.

"I'll quit my job after we're married," I tell him.

And after I see the prenup.

"So, we're all set," he says.

"Why didn't you tell me you were engaged to another woman?"

"It didn't seem important."

My brows rise. "Not important?"

"I know next to nothing about your past relationships," Stefan offers.

"That's because you said you don't want to know."

"I don't," he says.

"Well, I do. And for the record, I've never been engaged, before you."

Stefan's face softens. "If you must know, it was over children. Amelia wanted to postpone a family for her career. I was ready. So, we decided to go our separate ways. And that's why you"—he dots the tip of my nose with his index finger—"are perfect for me."

Then he exits the kitchen and heads toward his office.

Now the job-quitting comment makes more sense. His last fiancé picked career over family. It's not like I love my job or anything. But I don't like to be told what to do.

Following him, I continue. "Women have babies and careers, Stefan. They're not mutually exclusive. And it should be my choice."

"True," he says. "But things are different, marrying into this kind of money. You can't let your guard down. I need to protect my family."

That lands a little better with me, so I leave it for now.

I've tried to find out more about Amelia Summers, but she seems to have vanished off the face of the earth. I'd love to know what she's doing now, and why she walked away from a life like this. Most women wouldn't. Perhaps she had money of her own.

Or maybe she took a good look at the prenup and ran for her life. Maybe I would too—if it weren't for this baby. Because either way, I'm tethered to Stefan for the foreseeable future.

And a single mom from Bay Ridge is no match for a man like him.

TWENTY-ONE
ERIN

"Hey, Uncle Brody," I say.

We're meeting at a diner on the Lower East Side. Uncle Brody is my father's brother, and if I were to have a real wedding, he'd likely be the one to walk me down the aisle. He has an annoying habit of pinching me on the cheek every time we meet, but rather than complaining, I usually let him do it.

This time is no exception. "You're a peach, Erin Donovan." His stubby fingers reach over and sandwich my cheek flesh between them. It hurts a little, but I don't let on about it. He probably doesn't know his own strength.

Brody Donovan is a formidable man. Not tall, but broad and thick, with twinkly brown eyes, dark hair that has grayed some, and a rounded, ruddy face that makes him look younger than he is, which is early sixties.

"Your mother tells me you're engaged," he says. "To some rich kraut in the Hamptons."

I sigh. My working-class family has always been somewhat put off by my choices in life, so I let him get it out of his system for a while. He teases me a little, and I let him.

Because I need his help. Bay Ridge, where my father's family is from, has a large population of Russian immigrants. Not as large as Brighton Beach a few miles away, but it's all connected. And although New York City is a big place, it's not that big, and in the ethnic enclaves, it can sometimes operate more like a small town in terms of the word on the street.

Brody does business with the Russians in Brooklyn. Don't ask me what kind of business, because I don't want to know, and neither should you. But he knows people. And those people, even if they don't know Dimitri Petrov, they surely know of him. And I need someone I can trust to look into this, on the down-low.

Someone who is not a federal prosecutor.

So, I let him pinch my cheek and give me crap about my rich boyfriend. My accent shifts from prep school posh to Brooklyn street-smart. I'm a social chameleon when need be. I've been doing it most of my life.

"Uncle Brody," I say, my eyes wide and hopeful. "I need your help. I need you to look into someone for me."

He perks up at this.

The truth is, people like my Uncle Brody like to be useful. And although his business has some questionable elements, he's at heart a family man, and he'd do anything for me. My father was the black sheep of sorts, going his own way with the fire department. Staying out of the family business. But I've always known I could count on my family if the time came.

"Who? The kraut?" he says.

"No. Well, I guess a little. But no. There's someone else. A Russian."

He shakes his head. "Those guys are brutal. A mobbed-up Russian? You gotta stay away from guys like that, Erin."

"No, I don't think so," I say. "His name is Dimitri Petrov. He's an oligarch. In the Hamptons."

Uncle Brody rolls his eyes.

I fill him in on the rest of it.

Tanner.

The art forgery gone bad.

Stefan's family and his natural gas business.

"Look, Erin. I know you like this guy. And you've always gone after his type. But this time, it might be better to walk away. Find a regular rich guy. A VP. A banker. Just a regular guy with a good job. I don't like the sound of this."

I let out a sigh. "It's not that simple."

"I know. I was young once. A long time ago. I remember what it was like. But still—"

I hold up my hand. "No, that's not it, Uncle Brody. The truth is, I'm pregnant."

His eyes widen. "You're having a baby?"

I nod, and I'm afraid I'm going to get a lecture. They're all diehard Catholics, although I think it's more of a cultural than a spiritual commitment.

But that's not what happens.

Brody's eyes start to water, ever so slightly. He puts a hand on mine. "Your father was a great man," he says. "And I'll do everything in my power to protect his grandchild. When's the wedding? You better make it fast, Erin."

Seems to be a popular sentiment.

But I haven't told my mother yet about the elopement,

which is happening in a few weeks. It'll be less complicated if we just do it and tell people later.

"Soon," I say. "We're planning something intimate." Which is the truth, really. "You'll be one of the first to know."

"I'll be happy to walk you down the aisle. That is, if you want me to."

"That would be nice," I say, which isn't a total lie. It would be nice—if I weren't eloping. But still, I need to change the subject. I don't want to outright lie to my family.

See, Brody doesn't have any kids, and he and I have always been close. His wife Margaret died of cancer, way too early, and he never remarried. He still talks about her like she's alive, and I picture him walking around his house having conversations with her, as if she were still there with him. My mother was like that for a while, talking to my dad as if he was still there with us. Maybe it's an Irish thing. Mom has a gentleman friend now, but they've never talked about marriage. I asked her about it once, and here's what she said:

Your father is my husband, Erin.

Irish are like lobsters. We mate for life.

"So, you think you can find out anything about them? What does your gut tell you?"

"The brother and the art forgery's probably no big deal. But if there's money laundering going on, that could be dangerous."

I happen to know that he's right on both counts. Proving the origins of a work of art—the provenance, it's called—is a complex process fraught with problems. Most art sales are private, and even the authorities sometimes disagree on the authenticity of a piece. Plus, most experts are reluctant to challenge a provenance claim, for fear of being sued. What Tanner did is no big thing, I'm sure. But what concerns me more is Stefan convincing him to take a deal. What is he hiding if he didn't want the feds looking into it?

Because money laundering in contemporary art is another matter. It's a six-billion-dollar business, tied into all sorts of dangerous and ugly illegal dealings. The feds are cracking down, but it's hard to regulate private sales, kind of like guns. But then Stefan said he deals in old masters, not contemporary pieces, which I already told my uncle.

"I know. So, you'll check?" I ask.

"Let me get on this. Don't ask a lot of questions, Erin. Just keep your suspicions to yourself and play dumb. That's the best way to protect yourself until we learn more."

We say our goodbyes, but not before he gives me a small canister of pepper spray.

It's not the first time he's given me one, and he's warned me repeatedly about the dangers of a woman living alone in Manhattan. Usually, I brush it off. Make jokes. Tell him he worries too much. But this time, his words give me a shiver. Because now the threats, if there are any, are inside the walls, not outside of them.

"Be careful," he says.

And this time, all I do is nod.

TWENTY-TWO
MADISON

"I'm coming to the city for a meeting," I tell him. "I could meet you then, but I don't have much to report."

"That works," he says.

He gives me a location and hangs up.

Erin came through with the lead on the gallery owner. I got Jeremy to take two days of vacation so I could follow up on it, with the understanding I'd stipulate to the client that, until the kids go back to school, I'm only available to operate in a remote capacity. They've barely started on the structural renovations, so I'm sure it will be fine.

So, I'll kill two birds with one stone, starting with the meeting at the gallery.

The owner's name is Tina Weston. She seems like a badass bitch, and I mean that as a compliment. I'm sure we'll hit it off.

It's been a while since I've had a business meeting, and I know people are dressing down these days. Still, it's always better to be the best-dressed person in the room rather than the worst. Donning my white linen suit, I eye myself in the full-length mirror, agonizing over the shoes. I've tried on like twenty pairs. I land on a medium heel red pump to add a splash of color and move on to the jewelry. That's a little easier. A chunky platinum rope chain and some ruby studs. My hair is down, and I wonder if it isn't a bit too long. Oh, well. It will have to do for today. I look horrible with my hair up, and a ponytail is too casual.

I'm driving myself to the city, since I can't let anyone know about my second meeting. I'm usually excited, but today I have a strange stirring in my gut.

Is it guilt?

Is it fear?

Is it anticipation?

Probably a mix of these emotions.

The thought of going to work again, being able to stand on my own two feet, especially now that the kids are older, excites me. It would be a game changer. Already, Jeremy's showing me a little more respect. And I've realized that it would be best to extract myself from the Tanner situation.

But that's easier said than done. Still, maybe I can start to lay the groundwork for a graceful exit, if I can get this client under my belt. Taking a deep breath, I look in the mirror, square my shoulders and prepare myself for battle.

TINA WESTON IS, indeed, a badass bitch. I love her. She barks orders at the construction team like a mob boss—and they listen. She doesn't seem to be the least bit intimidated by them, dressed in black low-heeled pumps and a navy suit, her chestnut hair up in a chignon. I'm so glad I didn't dress down. That would have offended her, I'm sure. She's a little older than me. Married, but no kids. The kind of woman my mother would pity.

Mirroring her moxie, after we get the basics out of the way, I boldly assert that I can't start coming into the city on a regular basis until after Labor Day. Tina bristles, but then admits that she likely won't be ready for me until then, anyway.

"With a small retainer, I can hold that date for you," I say, pleased with myself and my gumption.

She arches a brow. My stomach sinks. "That's very generous of you, Madison," she says, her voice low and measured. "But I was planning to give you half up front. Isn't that standard practice in your field?" She pauses. And then she narrows her eyes at me. "Oh. That's right. You've been on the mommy track for the last decade." Then she sits back and crosses her arms.

And now I've overplayed my hand.

"You're absolutely right. I'm a little rusty. Half down would be fine too," I say. Then I offer her an apologetic shrug. I have a lot to learn, and Tina Weston seems like a good mentor.

As if reading my mind, she says, "I like you, Madison Bradford. But don't push your luck with me. I think this could work out well for both of us, as long as you play by my rules."

I nod. "Of course. We have a deal, then? I'd be eternally grateful for the opportunity."

"Yeah, yeah," she says. "We have a deal. Now please, see yourself out."

MY SECOND MEETING turns out to be even more fun than the first one.

"I told you already. I don't have much to report," I say.

He stares me down, and his silence is unsettling.

Does this guy ever blink?

"It doesn't have to be much," he says, finally. "Just give me what you've got."

I've thought carefully about this, about how much, if anything, to reveal. And I've decided to tell him some of it, but not all of it. Because he could be useful to me.

"Tanner suspects that Stefan framed him to cut him out of his inheritance." I explain the concept that Tanner mentioned, about compulsory estate law. I'm not sure if I pronounce it correctly, but I tell him the German word, as best I can remember:

Pflichtteil.

"Interesting. What do you think?" he asks.

"What do I know? You tell me. You're with the FBI. I'm just a Hamptons housewife."

"I think you underestimate yourself, Madison." Agent Nick Marino smirks, and this makes me tingle a little inside.

He's about my age with a sexy smile, jet-black hair, and a rough-and-tumble look that works for him, right out of central casting. He could play the lead in his own series.

I shrug. "Perhaps."

Inside, I smile back.

I hate to admit that I fall for the compliment, even though I know it's a tactic.

Then I continue. "At first, I thought Tanner might be on to something. But then he started to get almost... delusional."

"Delusional?" Marino asks.

I let out a huff, but it's only for show. "Oh, he thinks

Stefan might have murdered his younger brother. The one who died in a skiing accident. It's ridiculous, right? And Tanner's concerned that Stefan's last fiancé vanished after they broke up." I throw up my hands.

Marino's eyes widen, which is unusual for him.

Normally, the guy has a good poker face.

"Interesting," he says.

"Why is it interesting?" I ask.

"This is not a two-way street," Agent Marino says.

But he's already given me something. It's not out of the question, he thinks. I can tell by his reaction.

"Oh, well, what's a little gossip between friends?" I smile. "If you keep my secrets, I'll keep yours. I promise."

Basically, I'm being blackmailed by the federal government. Of course, Marino has never come out and said he'd out me about the affair with Tanner if I didn't cooperate. But the implied threat lingers in the background. Along with all of the photographs, which could easily be leaked to the media. I get a small fee for my informing, which I've been using to offset Jeremy's belt-tightening. And if I get the gallery account, I can extract myself from this arrangement.

Because the joke's on him. I don't care anymore if Jeremy knows about my affair. I might even tell him about it myself. Marino is interested in money laundering, not stolen art. He wants me to look out for some Russian guy named Dimitri Petrov and a possible connection with Stefan Ziegler.

Truth be told, I'm using Marino as much as he's using me. Because there are things I don't tell him. Like the fact that Tanner threatened to try and frame Stefan. Like the fact that there's a secret room in the Ziegler house, which I'm pretty sure is full of valuable old master paintings, which I overheard Stefan tell someone on the phone when I was in the guesthouse and he was outside by the pool, where Erin couldn't hear him.

If my hunch is correct, if they are... misrepresented. Then there are rewards. Some really big ones. As much as ten million for a missing Vermeer. Most not so big. And I don't know what I'd actually do if I found out for sure that Stefan was dealing in stolen artwork. Would I turn him in for a reward? Maybe, but not for a small one. For a big one? Perhaps.

But not if Stefan's a psychopath.

I'm not that stupid.

So, I threw Agent Marino a bone.

And Marino took it.

He's practically salivating.

"Good work," he says. "I'll check out that lead about the brother's death. What do you see in that idiot anyway?" he asks.

"Which one?" I say.

We both laugh.

Then he adds, "In the meantime, be careful, Madison."

"Sure," I say.

And I will. Because one thing my parents drilled into my head is that a woman of means has to be able to protect herself. And I'm not relying on anyone else for that, although it doesn't hurt to have a hot FBI agent watching my back.

Literally.

Because when I sneak a glance over my shoulder as I'm walking away, I catch a glimpse of Nick Marino checking me out.

I offer him a fluttery wave.

He blushes a little.

This brings a smile to my face.

I've never been on a private jet before. And I have to say, it doesn't suck. The interior is cream-colored leather. Soft and inviting. We enter, cocoon ourselves into the comfy over-stuffed chairs, and relax. No passengers bumping into me as I fight for overhead bin space. No cramming myself into a middle seat in coach, hoping that we don't get stuck on the runway if I have to use the bathroom before we take off, which always seems to happen, no matter how hard I try to avoid it.

I've never even flown first class before. I've walked through it, though. This is even better. And for the first time, I miss having the option to drink alcohol. A flute of champagne would be perfect right now. Instead, Stefan and I toast with sparkling water, in crystal rocks glasses. He's great like that. Thoughtful. I told him I don't mind if he drinks, but he said he's standing in solidarity with me.

Stefan's cell rings. He stands and walks toward the back of the plane. He answers in German. We're not in the air yet, but they've closed the doors. I hesitate for a split second, and then I pull up the translation app.

Uncle Brody wasn't able to put my mind at ease. It's not as if he turned up anything incriminating on Petrov or Stefan. It's more what he didn't find. They're both so secretive, and I'm still not convinced Stefan's on the up and up. Neither is Brody.

The app works a little better in this small space, but I can only hear one side of the conversation. Stefan says something about a buyer. There's a long pause. Then, he tells the person not to worry, because he has the paintings with him.

What paintings?

Stefan answers in the affirmative a few times.

Ja. Ja.

Alles ist gut.

Yes, it's all good.

Then he hangs up and comes to join me. I fumble with the phone, trying to hide the app, and it drops to the floor. It lands face up, so I kick it under the seat just before he sits.

That was way too close.

What am I doing? Spying on my future husband? The father of my child? So what if he's selling a few paintings and he didn't tell me anything about it. That's not weird, is it?

Who am I kidding.

It's weird.

But I put it all aside as we take off.

Stefan takes my hand. As if I'm a princess, he kisses it. Then he puts a hand on my belly. "Do you have something on your mind, Erin?" he asks.

Did he see the app?

Does he know I was listening in?

"No," I say. "Not really. Why do you ask?"

"You seem a little distant," he says.

"Just nervous, I guess. I'm not sure what to expect. What if your father doesn't like me?"

"What's not to like? He'll love you. Especially when we tell him about the baby."

My eyes widen. "He doesn't know?"

"No. I wanted to tell him in person. But we need to promise to raise the baby Catholic," Stefan says. "My father will insist."

I realize there's a lot we haven't talked about. I'm not very religious, but I suppose it would make my family happy, too. This is something we should have discussed, though, not something he should dictate, and I tell him this.

"We're discussing it now," Stefan says.

"No, we're not. You telling me is not a discussion."

To my surprise, his jaw stiffens. He doesn't apologize. His lips press tightly together, but he doesn't speak. Instead, he breathes in and out of his nose, like he's simmering inside. My body responds, a little prickle of fear running through me.

"What's wrong?" I ask.

Stefan doesn't answer. Instead, he stands and retrieves his briefcase from the overhead bin. While he's distracted, I grab my phone from under the seat and tuck it into my purse. He sits, pulls out some paperwork, and we settle in.

And I have no idea how to interpret what just happened.

***

I MUST HAVE FALLEN ASLEEP, because when I wake up, we're only about an hour or so from landing. As my eyes flutter open, I see Stefan smile at me. He brushes the hair from my face.

"Wake up, sleepyhead," he says.

Stretching up as far as my hands will go, I yawn, and it all comes rushing back to me. The unspoken tension in the air. The look I saw on Stefan's face after I pushed back on his directive to raise our baby Catholic. Whatever it was, he seems to be over it.

Did I imagine it?

Did I misinterpret what I saw?

Part of me wants to ask him about it, but I don't want to start this trip off on the wrong foot. It's curious, though. And totally unlike him. Because whenever I've pointed out something I didn't like about our relationship, he's always been so generous and apologetic, like when I told him he hadn't been attentive enough while he was away.

But this wasn't about us. This was about our child, and when the time is right, we're going to need to have a conversation about parenting. Perhaps he's going to be more of a control freak about his kid than I would have imagined.

It makes sense when I think about it. He cares about image. Tanner took a deal, Stefan claimed, so it wouldn't embarrass the family if the case went to trial. Stefan insisted that his child not be born out of wedlock. Stefan's father wants the baby to be raised Catholic.

Families with money have expectations.

Mom's voice again.

She warned me about this, just the other day, so why am I surprised?

But we can work it out.

And now is not the time.

For now, we smile and make small talk and he tells me

about all the lovely places we'll be going to visit. I wonder if he's playing some kind of game with me. Testing me, to see if I'll bring up our unborn child's religious education again. Or perhaps he considers the matter closed. We're touching down in Munich, so I suppose I'll find out soon enough.

I take a deep breath, swallow, and try to stay positive.

TWENTY-FOUR
ERIN

If a man's father is any indication of how he'll age, I am a lucky woman, indeed. Edmund Ziegler is a silver fox, if I've ever seen one. The resemblance to Stefan is uncanny, although I can see a little of Tanner in him around the eyes. The shape of his face, though, is all Stefan, along with his build. I expected him to be standoffish and guarded, but in terms of personality, he's quite genial when he greets us at the colossal front door. It is heavy and black and if it closed on your hand, it would probably remove it from your arm.

"Erin," he says, with a thicker German accent than his son, "I am most pleased to meet you. Stefan has told me so much about you. Come in."

The home is massive and stately. It looks more like something you'd see in the Loire Valley, like a French château: an off-white exterior with darker trim, Doric columns, and ornate but tasteful stone and metal work. Balconies extend around the upper floors, and although I have yet to stand on one, I imagine the views are spectacular from all vantage points, nestled as it is in the foothills of the Alps and surrounded by farmland as far as the eye can see.

It's on the cusp of fall. A slight chill whips in from the north, tempered by the warm sun when it peeks out from behind the clouds. The leaves are turning more here than at home, being further from the equator, as we are. No snow on the mountain tops, but still, it's breathtakingly beautiful.

We enter the large foyer with its parquet marble floor and move to a room which would be spacious in any other context, but I'm sure it's not the main living room. A waiter or butler or whoever he is comes and takes our drink orders. Stefan and his father chat in German, and I catch none of it.

Instead, I look around and absorb my surroundings. If it weren't for the high ceilings and large windows, it might look dated and staid, with the massive chandelier in the entryway, the heavy draperies, and the dark wood floor. But there's so much light, so much space around the furnishings that it appears at once traditional and modern. I have to say, it's one of the most magnificent dwellings I've ever seen.

After a few minutes, my ears perk up.

Stefan said something to his father about the paintings.

Maybe it's my body language, or the fact that they've been excluding me for so long they finally sense that they're bordering on rude. They turn their attention to me and shift to English—and say nothing further about it.

Okay.

What's the big deal?

Why does this bother me so much?

Stefan does some art deals.

Perhaps he procured a few paintings for his father, or one of his father's friends.

So what?

I try to convince myself that it means nothing. But then why is he being so secretive about it, if he has nothing to hide?

"Erin," Stefan repeats. "My father asked how the trip was."

"Oh," I reply. "Sorry," I say, realizing I've been spacing out. "I'm a little jet lagged. It was fine. I mean, it was lovely. Just perfect. And your home is spectacular."

"I hope you will be comfortable here," he says. "But Stefan tells me you are headed to the South of France, only staying for a few days." He doesn't look pleased about this. "We will barely have time to get acquainted."

I turn to Stefan.

Stefan takes a deep breath. "About that. We have some news. The timeline has changed for the wedding. Because Erin is, we are, having a baby."

Edmond's eyes widen and his mouth hangs open.

Stefan and I don't dare utter a word.

After what feels like a very long time, he speaks.

"Das ist... wunderbar," he says. "Wonderful. I wish your mother was here to share this welcome news with us." Edmond pats Stefan on the back, a hearty slap, as if celebrating his virility.

We discuss the good news as the butler returns with our drinks. It's late afternoon, and his father is having what appears to be whisky or scotch, neat.

Stefan has followed suit.

So much for the solidarity.

I'm having sparkling water, and I'm getting pretty sick of it.

After a half hour or so of small talk about me, my family,

and how we met, Stefan mentions that we'd like to get settled in our room. I'm grateful for this. I could use a shower and maybe a nap, although a part of me wants to charge out and see the sights. We only have a few days.

"What do you want to see while you're here?" Edmond asks.

"Stefan suggested the Neuschwanstein Castle, and maybe Rothenburg, if we have time. But we're mainly here to see you, so that is our priority."

"Nonsense. Make the most of your time. My days are full with work, so do not concern yourself with my needs. Is there anything else you'd like to see?" Stefan's father asks.

"Well, we're pretty close to Dachau," I say. "Would that be worth a look? Have you been?"

Stefan's jaw drops, and he looks at me like I've lost my mind. "Erin! Why would you suggest something so... unpleasant?"

"It's... never mind," I say. "You're right. It's not that kind of trip. I've just heard a lot about it, that's all." To call a concentration camp unpleasant is perhaps the understatement of the century, but I let that go.

"Well," his father says. "I suppose we should be happy that Neuschwanstein wasn't bombed into oblivion during the war, so you'll have something more pleasant to tour. Now, I have business to attend to. Make sure to be home by three tomorrow for our meeting with the attorney."

The one about the prenup.

With that, he leaves us sitting alone. I knew about Neuschwanstein, from my art education. It's a late nineteenth-century castle built by the mad King Ludwick II, and it was also the model for the Disney castle, which I never got to see in person as a child. The Nazis stored their looted artwork there because it was so remote; they figured it would be spared from the bombing raids, which it was. But most of the stolen art was recovered during the occupation.

"What were you thinking, Erin?" Stefan barks at me.

"I'm sorry," I say.

Although, I'm not sure what I should be sorry about. Dachau is on all the lists of the top tourist attractions in Bavaria. It's not like I'm the only person on the planet who's ever thought of touring it. I know that Germans can be a little defensive about the war years, but I wasn't expecting such strong pushback. Still, I suppose is a little inappropriate to visit such a place on this trip, considering we're here to get married. So, I let it go, but Stefan doesn't.

"The occupation was hard on Germany," he says. "Most people don't know much about that, nor do they care. Our family suffered. First trying to stay out from under Nazi control, and then after the war ended. It's a sore spot."

I let out a sigh.

Of course it is a sensitive topic, and not just in the abstract.

I never thought about it. And now I feel terrible.

"Do you want to talk about it?" I ask.

"I do not," he says.

And with that, we head to our suite without another word about it.

I realize now I need to keep my mouth shut. Sit back. Listen and observe. Because there's something odd about this family. And since I'm soon to be one of them, I need to find out what it is.

Trying not to let myself think the worst, I fail miserably, as dark thoughts seep into my psyche. Stefan says they tried to stay out from under Nazi control during the war years.

But what else is he going to say? And his father seemed so enthused about our surprise news. I place my hand on my belly, feeling a little protective.

What is going on with this family?

And do I even want to know?

TWENTY-FIVE
MADISON

I've been avoiding Tanner. Erin and Stefan are in Europe visiting his family, and I could conceivably be at his place a lot more than I have been, without fear of being caught. But the truth is, he's starting to get on my nerves, and the guilt is getting to me. I can't ignore him forever, though, so here I am, knocking on the front door of his cottage.

"Madison," Tanner calls out from the main house. "I'm in here."

I make my way to the French doors to enter the house from the backyard. Tanner grabs me and pulls me in for a steamy kiss before I can get a word out.

"The cameras," I say. "I'm not an exhibitionist.

"I turned the system off," he says. "Relax."

Tanner pulls me back into his embrace, and I have to admit, he's got the magic touch. If only he'd keep his mouth shut. I could ask him to role-play. Pretend he doesn't speak English or something. Still, my marriage is effectively dead, so I close my eyes and let my body respond, and it does.

Soon, Tanner's hands are massaging me in all the right

places. He leads me to the sofa. I close my eyes and let my mind drift as I sink into it. After we finish, Tanner springs up and tells me he's got a dentist appointment. He's gotten permission to leave for that, as long as he phones in and doesn't deviate from the plan.

"I'll be back in a few hours. You can stay if you want. It's kinda hot, thinking of you, waiting here for me."

I want to ask him if he's found out any more about his inheritance, or if he's gotten anywhere on his plan to have Stefan arrested, but I can't hit that head-on. So, I try a more roundabout line of questioning.

"Have you heard anything from Stefan about how it's going over in Europe?"

"No, why would he tell me anyway?"

I shrug. "True. So, when you said you wanted to get Stefan arrested. Are you saying he's doing something illegal?"

He shakes his head. "I was just blowing off steam. I'm not going to do anything like that, Maddie. Forget it, okay? I'm going to do my time. Fight for what's mine. And go back to L.A. where I belong. This town is boring, and I want to act again."

My brow furrows. "Okay, but..."

"Oh, shit, babe," Tanner says, and his hand goes to his forehead. "That was so insensitive of me." He comes over, tucks a stray hair behind my ear, and cradles my chin. "But we both knew this was temporary, right? I mean, I really like you, but..." He shrugs.

This is fantastic.

I can't believe my luck.

Pressing my lips together to keep the corners of my mouth from lifting up into a telling grin, I attempt to look wounded. "I get it, Tanner. It's just so hard, you know? Thinking about you leaving. Giving up what we have."

My head tilts to one side, and I put on my sad girl face.

"I know, babe. We've got a few months, so let's make the most of it."

"But won't that make it even harder to let go?" I ask. "Maybe we should just..."

He holds up a hand, likely knowing it might be even worse here without his conjugal visits. "Let's not make any decisions now, okay? You never know what might happen. I might be able to get an acting gig in New York. Who knows what the future holds?"

But I know that's total bullshit. Tanner's using me as much as I'm using him. I need to stay one step ahead of him, though. So, I bat my eyes and say, "Right. Let's take it one day at a time."

"That's my girl. Now, I gotta bounce. See you soon. Stay put, okay?"

He pats me on the ass and I nod.

After watching him leave, I make my move.

Because I'm going to get something out of this—before I cut him off completely and end this bizarre chapter of my life.

THE SECRET ROOM might be a myth. Perhaps I didn't hear Stefan correctly. Because I've been looking for his secret storage room for the last hour. The one I overheard him talking about. My grandfather was German, and I can understand some of what Stefan says on the phone. But I'm rusty, and his dialect is different. And I have yet to find a room full of old master paintings.

Tanner turned off the cameras; so now is my chance, and if I don't find it today, I probably won't get a second try. I'm planning to end it with Tanner when he comes home. No sense in dragging it out, especially if I find what I'm looking for.

I've done some research, and I know that the room would likely be climate-controlled, so that means it has to be fairly large. I'm thinking a bookcase is too obvious for someone who has such a high-stakes situation, so I'm looking for something a bit more subtle. Mirrors or panels that seem out of place, for example. And some kind of mechanism to trigger it. Some systems use biometrics, and that would be unfortunate, because if that's the case, there's a good chance that even if I locate the room, I might not be able to get in.

Stefan's office looks larger from the outside than the inside, so I'm back here, the first place I looked, trying to see if I'll have better luck this time. Holding a grill lighter to the cracks in the wall panels, I check to see if air is coming through. The flame flickers a little in front of the panel on the wall that backs up to his bedroom closet.

My heart starts to race, and I realize that I have no idea what I'll do if I actually find something.

What could be the trigger, if this is the room?

I look around and start manipulating objects.

A floor lamp.

A vase.

A painting on the wall.

Nothing.

This is crazy, I tell myself.

I should quit while I'm ahead.

And then I see it.

A notch in the baseboard, just behind the floor lamp.

I would not have noticed it if I hadn't moved the lamp.

I step on it with my foot, and a door creaks open. It's about half the size of a normal door, so I'll need to crouch down to enter.

For a few minutes, I reconsider.

Do I want to go down this road?

But curiosity gets the better of me.

I step in.

The room is dark, so I can't see much.

When my eyes adjust, I notice five crates that look to be the right size and shape for paintings, but what good will this do? I can't very well pry them open. I have no idea if they're stolen. For all I know, they could be tied to Stefan's legitimate business.

I have a sudden urge to flee.

Before I do, I snap a few photos to send off to Agent Marino.

The floorboards creak, and the hairs on the back of my neck stand up.

"Somebody's been a bad kitty," a voice says.

The door slams shut, leaving me in total darkness.

TWENTY-SIX
ERIN

The prenup was surprisingly generous in terms of the money, but there were some elements that gave me pause, and I wouldn't be surprised if it sent his last girlfriend packing. I emailed a copy to my mother, who hired an attorney to look it over.

The financial terms I won't contest. As long as I don't cheat, I'm fine. The only way I can be left virtually penniless is if he invokes the infidelity clause. I have to wonder if that's mostly a lineage issue, since the entire family seems obsessed with our future child, or children, as they seem to assume they'll be more than one.

There are stipulations about the education of the children, about raising them Catholic, and using "appropriate parenting," which seems to suggest that if I don't meet the family's standards in terms of mothering, Stefan can get full custody. Again, the finances are not an issue. They seem unconcerned about money, and as long as I don't sleep with another person, I'll never want for anything again.

But the idea of losing control of my children?

Not being able to parent as I see fit?

The thing is, these people have resources. Even if I don't sign the prenup and I don't marry Stefan, they could still take my child away. Stefan has dual citizenship. He could take my baby and leave the country. Go somewhere without an extradition treaty. So, no matter what the attorney says, I think I'm stuck having to sign it.

Stefan claims it's all just a formality. He says that we will be co-parents and he's happy to defer to me on most matters. But what else is he going to say?

But we're getting married today, a civil procedure to obtain our marriage license. Then it's off to the South of France, for our elopement and a honeymoon.

After I sign the prenup.

I haven't told my mother yet, and I feel terrible about that. Stefan went for a run, and I'm mulling it over. I still have a chance to make it right. As if reading my mind, she calls.

"Erin?" she says.

"Mom! How are you?"

"This agreement, it's... ridiculous," she says. I can see her tapping her foot on the floor. "Totally ridiculous. You can't sign it. I won't stand for it."

"Is that what the attorney said?"

"No, that's what I'm saying. I'm your mother, Erin. I don't give a damn what some attorney woman says. You need to fight this."

The attorney probably feels like I do; that if I don't marry him, I'm in even graver danger of losing control of my child. But Mary Donovan is a firebrand of a woman. A Pitbull. She sort of looks like one, too. Short and stout with light brown hair and a pleasant face—unless you piss her off. Fiercely protective of her own.

One time when I was about seven, an older mean girl was bullying me on the playground. My mother threatened to break her kneecaps. She's lucky nobody was around to hear her say it. But I have to admit, the girl never bothered me again.

I explain my theory. That not signing it, and not marrying him, would be way worse.

"That's what the attorney said. That wimp." In my mind's eye, she's shaking her head.

Obviously, I can't tell my mom that I'm eloping. She'll be devastated. But right now, I have a child to think about, and he is my priority.

Yes, we found out the gender.

I'm having a boy.

A boy who will inherit a noble lineage, a fortune, and a ton of baggage.

And I can't help but think that my mother was right. Being a rich guy's wife is, already, not what I anticipated, and I haven't even married the guy yet.

But I know what I need to do. Mom admits to me that the attorney thinks I should sign it. Because if it ever came to blows, the courts would likely overturn it, especially in a custody case. Mom said she emailed me her full report. This makes me feel a lot better, so I tell Mom I need to go so I can read it.

"Mom. Why didn't you lead with that?" I ask.

"Because this is bullshit, Erin."

Mom hardly ever swears.

And she's right.

It is bullshit.

But what choice do I have?

"I need to go, Mom. I love you."

"I love you, too, honey. And don't take any crap from that kraut. You can still get out of this. We're all here for you."

This makes me feel supported, although I don't think she's right about that. I'll be better off married, rather than trying to fight Stefan and his family as a single mother. The report leaves me feeling better. The attorney said the provisions are virtually unenforceable in an American court, and she would know.

Stefan comes back from his workout, looking adorable with his hair all messy. Trying to stay positive, I decide to give him the benefit of the doubt. I mean, when push came to shove, Harry chose Meghan over the royal family. Perhaps I can trust him when he says it's just a formality.

"We need to get ready," Stefan says.

"Not so fast," I say. "We've got one more item on the agenda before we leave."

He flashes me a sexy grin. "Well, I think it's more traditional to consummate the marriage after the ceremony, but I'm game if you are."

I shake my head. "No, silly. The prenup. I need to sign it."

His head tilts to one side. "You're sure?"

"I'm sure," I say.

I'm sure that an American court of law would render it unenforceable.

"I love you," he says. "It's just a formality. I promise."

"I love you, too."

With that, I sign the paperwork and head into the

shower, hopeful that that's the last I ever see of our prenuptial agreement, and trying with all my heart to believe what he just said.

Because I'm pretty sure that without trust, our love is doomed.

Oh my God.

Oh my God.

It's so dark, I feel like I'm being buried alive.

My heart starts to race, and I struggle to slow it before I have a full-blown panic attack.

What if he never lets me out?

What if the house catches on fire?

I'm going to die a slow death inside these walls, like something out of a horror movie.

"Tanner!" I cry out. "Let me out of here. I can explain."

My phone dropped to the floor in all the commotion, so I bend down and pat my hands around to try and find it. There's probably no cell service in here, but if I can get some light, that would help.

No luck.

"Tanner!" I scream his name.

And I keep screaming it, over and over and over.

"Help! Someone help me! Please!"

My voice is getting hoarse, and I'm wearing myself out.

Now it feels like my throat is closing up.

I need water.

What if I die of thirst in here?

How long does that take?

Finally, I find the phone and pull up the flashlight app. It doesn't help much, because now I can see how fucked I am, stuck in this room, completely at Tanner's mercy.

"I'm trying to help you!" I plead. "I heard Stefan talking about this room. I wanted to see if I could find something to help you put him away."

Finally, Tanner speaks. "Calm down, Maddie. I'm not a psychopath. Just tell me how to open the door. We don't need the cops showing up, so you have to promise to stop screaming."

Tanner didn't know about this room?

I'm still shaky and my palms are sweaty, but I'm starting to calm down. "I'll stop, I promise. Just let me out. Look for the notch in the baseboard, behind the lamp."

Soon, the door opens.

I catapult out the opening with the force of a hurricane.

Tanner is standing with his arms folded, smiling. I pummel the smug bastard with my fists, breathing through my nose. I swear, if I had a weapon, I could kill him right now. He has no idea who he's dealing with.

He lifts me up by my shoulders, asserting his dominance, totally amused by my lame show of force. "Aren't you a feisty little minx? I was just having a little fun with you."

"You call that fun? Entombing me in a wall?"

"Why do you have to be such a drama queen? You're fine. But I'm going to need an explanation. What the hell were you doing in there?"

Suddenly, I start laughing like a madwoman. It comes

out of nowhere, and I'm at a loss for how to stop it. Maybe that's what happens when your life flashes before your eyes. I'm practically convulsing, laughing, and crying at the same time.

Because it's all too much. This isn't me. I was a good girl for most of my life. I followed the rules. Obeyed my parents. Did my homework. Married well. What am I doing, getting myself locked in a closet by a convicted felon? Being blackmailed by the FBI?

I need to pull myself together.

Tanner just stares at me.

Finally, I get a grip. "You weren't going to leave me in there forever?"

"No. Of course not. But like I said, I need an explanation."

"And I need a drink."

Charging into the living room, I down a shot of vodka.

Then I explain to him what I overheard.

"And why didn't you tell me so we could go looking for the room together?" he asks.

"I wasn't sure what it meant. And I thought maybe it was a stupid idea. But then you said the cameras were off. And it's the only time I've been here alone, and I didn't have to worry about Stefan coming home. So I figured I'd look around. And of course, if I found anything, I planned to tell you. But then you came back. Why were you so early, anyway? You said you'd be a few hours."

"I turned the cameras back on when I left," he says, eyeing me.

"You were spying on me? Was this some kind of test?"

He narrows his eyes at me. "If it was, you failed miserably."

Tanner's not as dumb as he looks.

This isn't making me look any better, so I try a different tactic. "Okay, well, when you said you were going back to L.A., it really shook me up, Tanner. I was hoping that if I could help you get something on your brother, then maybe..."

Tanner has a big ego. I can tell he wants to believe this.

He sighs. "I'm sorry. What I said didn't come out right."

I'm not great at faking it when it comes to romance. Soon, he'll realize that I'm full of crap, but I think I've got some time. Right now, I just want to get out of here without arousing any more suspicion.

So, I let him go on about how he's going to figure out a way to look inside those crates and see if there's anything he can use to frame Stefan. I let him think that all I wanted was to lead him to the paintings and try to get him to stay with me. Then I tell him I need to get back to my family.

And that's the only true thing I've said since he let me out of the storage room.

Before I can make my exit, we are interrupted by a knock on the door. Tanner peeks out the window. "It's the cops," he says. "They probably heard you yelling. Nice going!"

"Tell them it was the TV," I say, and I run into the kitchen to hide.

There's a large walk-in pantry that seems to be my only option. After being locked in that storage room, this is the last thing I need. But what choice do I have? I can't be caught here at their house. I know I said I was ready to tell Jeremy, even flaunt it in his face, but I'm not ready. I have my kids to think about. They need to be my priority from now on.

"What's this about?" Tanner asks.

I can hear them, but barely. They're in the foyer, just off the kitchen.

"We'd like to speak to Stefan Zeigler," an officer says.

Thank goodness. They're not looking for a screaming woman. This has nothing to do with me. I breathe a sigh of relief.

The officer is a man, and he sounds older, like he's someone experienced, with an air of authority in his voice, which makes me think that this could be something serious.

"He's in Europe," Tanner says.

"We have a few questions for you," the officer says.

For Tanner?

Why Tanner?

This can't be good.

"What do you know about an Amelia Summers?"

My stomach sinks.

It's the same officer, but I'm pretty sure there's two of them, based on the footsteps.

"She's Stefan's old girlfriend. Or fiancé, I guess," Tanner says.

"You tell me," a female officer says.

Her voice is on the sultry side, and I picture one of those women detectives you see on TV, sporting skintight jeans and a plunging neckline that no actual woman would ever wear to a job like that.

"There's not much to tell," Tanner says. "Amelia Summers was engaged to my brother. About a year and a half ago, they broke it off. She moved out. That's about all I know. Why are you asking?" Tanner says.

"She's dead," the woman says.

My pulse thrums in my ears.

I grab the wall to steady myself.

This is the last thing I need right now.

Dead?

"Oh, that's terrible," Tanner says. "I didn't know her very well, but still. She was so young. I moved here right at the tail end of their relationship. I'm sure Stefan will be devastated. But I'm not sure why you want to talk to my brother. He's engaged to another woman. As far as I know, they haven't been in contact since she left."

"Your brother may have been the last person to see her," the woman says.

"I guess I'm mistaken then. Maybe they're still friends. What do I know?"

"No," the male cop says. "According to our investigation, your brother may have been the last person to see her, a year and a half ago. When she was murdered. And dumped in a marsh not too far from here. We found her body a few days ago, and we just got a positive ID."

"Murdered?" Tanner says. "You can't think my brother had anything to do with this."

"Now why would you go and think that?" the woman asks.

Tanner stammers, "I, um, no, of course. Why are you here, then?"

"Just following the evidence," she says. "So you were living here when she was still with your brother. Maybe *you* were the last person to see her alive?"

"Me? No. I was working a lot back then. In the city. Before... this happened."

I picture Tanner pointing to the ankle monitor.

He continues. "I came home one day and she was gone. Stefan said they broke off the engagement."

"Right," she says. "Any idea why they broke it off?"

"Something about the prenup got her upset," Tanner says. "And the fact that she wanted to focus on career over starting a family. That's about all I know. She refused to sign the prenup. And my brother. Well, let's just say he doesn't like it when things don't go his way."

"Are you saying your brother has a temper?" the male cop asks.

"Everyone has a temper, when prompted," Tanner says.

"Even you?" the woman cop asks.

"Do I need an attorney?" Tanner asks.

"I don't know," she says. "Do you?"

"I'm not answering any more of your questions. And if I'm not under arrest, I'd like you to leave. Now."

"If that's how you want to play it," the male officer says.

"That's how I want to play it."

With that, Tanner sees them out.

And this time, I'm not so eager to come out of my hiding place.

I'm late, and I'll have to think up an excuse for Jeremy. But that's the least of my worries. This situation is more than I bargained for, and for the first time, this isn't a game to me anymore. There's a good chance I'm putting myself and my family in danger, which isn't at all what I signed on for. I need to extract myself from it.

My mind reels as I hold my head in my hands. "She's dead? *Dead?* What do they think happened to her? Who do you think killed her?"

"I don't know," Tanner exclaims. "They want to talk to him. Stefan told me she left."

"How are the police just finding out about this now? Wouldn't someone have reported her missing a year and a half ago?"

"Amelia didn't have much family, as far as I know. She was from somewhere in the Midwest. Came here to get into theater. That's about all I know." Tanner shrugs.

"Okay, I have to get home. What are you going to do

about the paintings? Maybe it's too dangerous to take it any further," I say.

Tanner nods. "Yeah, I've got bigger problems. I'll talk to my attorney. Clear my name. I was in the city the day Amelia moved out, so I can easily eliminate myself as a suspect."

My brow furrows. "Why would you be a suspect?"

He blows out a breath. "There's something nobody knows. And you can't tell anyone. Amelia and I were sleeping together. And I'm pretty sure Stefan knew."

My eyes nearly pop out of my head. "What? Was it serious?"

"No," he says. "I just did it to fuck with Stefan and mess up their relationship. I wasn't that into her. But she liked me more than she liked him. And she didn't want to sign that prenup. But now do you believe me? My brother is not who he pretends to be, I'm telling you. I'm glad they found her body. I'm probably safer now. He's not going to murder me with the cops up his ass for this."

"You might have a point."

"Sorry I dragged you into this, Maddie. And I don't blame you if you want out."

"Speaking of out..."

Hiking my thumb toward the back door, I tell Tanner I need to go. Then I bolt over to my house, struggling to come up with an excuse that explains where I've been, and realizing that the truth might be my best option.

WHEN I GET HOME, they've already left for Abby's tennis match. Jeremy isn't angry when I arrive at the club in the middle of her last set. He's sad, and this confounds me. I haven't seen my husband look this dejected since his mother died, over ten years ago.

"What's wrong?" I ask.

"Do you even have to ask?"

"I got held up at—"

"Save it, Madison," he says. "We need to talk."

"Yes, we do. But not here."

It's the one thing we agree on, so we put aside our issue and focus on the game. Abby wins, so at least I get to see the smile on her face, which quickly evaporates when she sees me. Daggers shoot from her eyes to mine. I feel like the worst mother on the planet, and I don't even make excuses.

"I'm sorry," I say. "And congratulations."

I drive home alone, and seeing the kids hop into the car with Jeremy, it crosses my mind that if I keep going in the direction I'm headed, I could lose everything. This could be my life. Me. Alone. With my family driving away from me.

WHEN WE GET the kids fed and they settle into their rooms for some downtime, Jeremy and I finally face each other.

"What's going on?" he says.

And I tell him some of it. How I felt taken for granted and worthless and unimportant. How his condescending jabs at my career aspirations hurt me. How we only have this house because of my inheritance. How meeting Tanner made me feel alive again. How Agent Marino approached me and wanted me to inform for him, and keep tabs on Stefan and Tanner.

And finally, I tell him about Amelia's murder, the inheritance squabbles, and the fact that Tanner thinks Stefan killed her.

Jeremy's jaw drops. "Holy shit, Madison. I mean, I figured it out, about your affair. But the rest of it? I think I need a moment," he says.

I study my husband's face, trying to gauge his level of shock.

He paces around the kitchen, running his hand through what's left of his hair.

"I know. It's a lot," I say.

Jeremy's brows rise. "You really think Stefan could have murdered his fiancé?"

I find it interesting that he doesn't use her name.

"Honestly, I don't know. It could have been a robbery gone bad," I say.

"Have you called this Marino guy and filled him in?"

"Not yet," I say. "I had to get to the tennis match."

Jeremy widens his eyes. "Call him now," he says. "Tell him you want out. We need to protect our family. What if they find out you're informing? What if we have murderers living next door?"

Truthfully, I'm dying to call Marino, but I don't want to do it in front of Jeremy. "I... can't," I lie. "We have set times I'm supposed to check in. It would be weird. And I'm sure he already knows about the murder."

Jeremy eyes me, but he lets it go.

I expect him to lay into me for all of it, but he doesn't.

Instead, he throws me a curveball. "So, what about us?" he says.

"What *about* us?" I reply. "I'm not sure there even is an 'us' anymore."

He sighs. "Do you think there could be?" he asks. "If we try?"

I let out a sigh. "I don't know."

I'm not sure what I expected would happen if Jeremy found out. I suppose I thought he'd be angry. But he's not. He looks hurt, which seems strange to me.

Because after all, he started it.

"Do you want to try?" he asks.

"I don't know what I want right now. I need some time alone."

And with that, I head upstairs to get my burner and call Marino.

We shared a magical first day as a married couple. The ceremony was at Castle Hill, a park dating back to the Middle Ages, and it was fairy-tale perfect, even without any guests. At midday, it was warm enough to go without a coat or jacket. We had a Roman Catholic priest as our officiant. Stefan said it would smooth things out with his father, and I'm sure it will placate my mother, once we come clean.

I wore a long, lacy, white strapless dress that hugged my curves. I'm not showing yet, which is one reason I wanted to do the ceremony sooner rather than later. Stefan wore a navy suit with a light blue striped tie that matched the powder blue Mediterranean Sea in the distance.

Our vows were short and sweet, because it's a touristy spot; we actually got a round of applause from the onlookers, who our wedding planner graciously held back long enough for us to share an intimate moment.

After taking some great photos by the ruins, the water-fall, and the lush gardens, we headed back to the hotel where we promptly consummated our marriage. I'm not sure if it was the excitement of being husband and wife, or perhaps it was the pregnancy hormones. But the sex was, well, like nothing I've experienced before, with Stefan or anyone else. It felt steamy and romantic, powerful yet tender, as if our hearts and souls and bodies were merging as one. I know that sounds corny, but it's the truth.

Afterward, Stefan surprised me with a private tour of the Chagall Museum, which I didn't even know was possible. It was a Tuesday, and it's supposed to be closed. It was so cute because he pretended to argue with me about it, insisting that I didn't know what I was talking about. I pulled it up on my phone, trying to show him, but he kept up the charade, acting dismissive. Which pissed me off, of course—but made the surprise even better.

"You rat!" I said, and batted him on the arm.

He flashed a cheeky smile, and we proceeded to get the royal treatment.

Later, I actually called my mother and fessed up, and Stefan told his dad. We chatted with both of them on the phone. Sent them the short wedding video so they'd be the first to see it. Assured them that we'd have a party in a few months.

They both took it well, although my mother isn't the type to voice her concerns to Stefan, a man she's never met. I might get an earful when she has me alone.

Then we went out to dinner in nearby Monte Carlo, at the only four-star Michelin restaurant in the vicinity, and dined on the most scrumptious meal I've had since the pregnancy. The morning sickness has subsided, and I have more of an appetite now.

It was the perfect wedding, that's for sure.

Too bad I'm not as sure about the marriage.

It's early morning, my second day as a married woman, and it started out fine. The first thing Stefan did was reach for me again. The lovemaking was a repeat of the day before. And for a while, all my worries and fears and suspicions evaporated. I let my mind go wild with little girl fantasies. I'd met my Prince Charming. I was going to have the life I've always dreamed of. And afterward, he looked deep into my eyes and said:

"Erin, I love you. And our baby. You've made my life complete. I never thought I'd find love again. And then I met you."

Find love *again?*

What the hell did that mean?

He kissed me, and I had to remind myself to kiss him back, because I was still focused on what he said. Then he sprung up and headed into the shower, leaving me lying here in our marital bed, wondering once again if I was a substitute for that ex of his.

Amelia.

Stefan said he was struck by the lightning bolt when he saw me at the bar that night.

Madison said we look alike.

Was it me, or the fact that I look like his ex?

His ex who, I'm pretty sure, based on what I just heard, dumped him and left him heartbroken?

We're leaving tomorrow, so I should probably try to make the best of my time here. I mean, so what if he has a type? Maybe he was first drawn to me because of the resemblance, but that doesn't mean I'm a substitute for her. I'm his wife now. The mother of his child. Even if she reappeared and tried to win him back, he's mine now. Still, the thought of being second fiddle bothers me. It bothers me a lot.

So much so that when he comes back, I ask him about it.

His brow furrows. "What?" he says. "I didn't say that. I said I never thought I'd find a love like this."

"No, Stefan," I insist. "You said you thought you'd never find love again."

He shakes his head, but more in a puzzled way rather than as an act of denial. "Perhaps it's my English. It's not what I meant. Can we please drop this and enjoy ourselves? You're the love of my life. The mother of my child. Isn't that enough for you?"

"Sure," I say, through my tightly pressed lips.

Because I know what I heard.

And I know when I'm being gaslit.

WE GOT THROUGH THE DAY, and we're headed to bed. We made the most of it. Toured the Matisse Museum, but with all the other visitors, which was fine. We fly back first thing in the morning, and I'm trying hard not to let that comment of his get to me.

It's stupid. He's right. I have a type. Why can't he? I've loved before. We all have. It's no big deal—although I have to question the timing of his comment, because you really don't want another woman on your man's mind while you're still technically making love.

Stefan's getting ready for bed when my cell buzzes with a text from Lucy. I ended up telling her about the elopement before I left. She's probably texting me a congratulations, although I didn't tell her exactly when we were tying the knot.

I open my phone and click on the text.

Sorry to dump this on you. The police
found Stefan's ex. She was murdered.
Over a year ago. Hold off on the wedding if
you can.

Gasping for air, I feel like the breath has been knocked out of me, like I forgot how to breathe after a punch to the gut. Like the ground beneath my feet is shifting, although I'm not standing up.

Sitting perfectly still on the edge of the bed, I stare at the message, wondering what the hell I've gotten myself into. I place a protective hand on my belly as my pulse starts to pound. And I'm seized with a fear so visceral, I feel as if I'm facing down a serial killer wielding a carving knife.

It's clear to me now that I don't know the man in the bathroom of our hotel suite very well, if at all.

The controlling prenup.

The connection to Dimitri Petrov.

The felonious brother.

And now this?

His last girlfriend was murdered?

Why does Lucy know this?

Do they think Stefan has something to do with it?

I glance down at my phone.

Lucy's read my mind.

Stefan is wanted for questioning. They've
already been to his house.

He must know about the murder, if they've been trying to reach him.

And he kept it from me.

I text Lucy back.

> Coming home tomorrow. I need to go now.
> He's coming.

Lucy replies:

> Pretend you know nothing until you get
> back. Erase these texts.

I do as she says.

"I'm tired," Stefan says, and he plops down next to me.

I place the phone face down on the dark wooden nightstand.

Relieved that he doesn't want to make love, I roll over and try to sleep, knowing that it will be hard. I have to try, though, for my baby boy.

All of this stress is taking a toll on my body, I can feel it.

Curling up on my side, I try to breathe myself to a healthier place, praying for sleep to come and the morning sun to rise, so I can get out of here and figure out what the hell to do next.

THE MARRIAGE

THIRTY-ONE
ERIN

"There's something I have to tell you," Stefan says, placing his hand on mine.

We're on the plane, about an hour or so from landing, and it's been a struggle to keep up appearances. I'm not feeling very well, so I'm hiding my fear and apprehension behind my physical symptoms. I'm sick to my stomach. I told Stefan it was morning sickness, although this feels different. I'm sure it's all the stress and anxiety.

He's probably going to tell me about Amelia. I feel so ill, I don't really have the energy to be angry. All I can muster is, "What is it?"

Stefan takes a deep breath. "This is going to be hard. I found out a few days ago, but I didn't want to spoil our trip. You're going to find out soon enough, though, so I'd like to get it out of the way now."

You kept it from me so you wouldn't ruin our trip?

Or so I wouldn't call off the wedding?

I fight the urge to shout out to him that I already know, but I can't. Because then I'd have to out Lucy and Justin.

And tell Stefan that the feds are watching him. He'd be furious that I've kept this from him for so long, and I realize now that I'm stuck. I can't come clean and tell him what I know and start our marriage out right. Even if he's innocent, our union is already tainted with secrets and lies of omission, on both of our parts.

"My ex. The one I was with before you. She was found dead."

"Oh, Stefan. That's terrible." Pausing for dramatic effect, as if I'm hearing this for the first time, I respond accordingly. "But... how did you hear about it?"

"This is hard, Erin. And you have to believe me, I had nothing whatsoever to do with this. But Amelia was murdered. And the police want to talk to me."

I continue. "To you? You were in Europe. With me. Why would anyone think you had something to do with it?"

"Because she was murdered over a year ago. They just found the body. I may have been the last person to see her alive, aside from... well, aside from whoever killed her. They're meeting us when we land."

What the hell?

They must have something on him.

How would a new, previously unsuspecting wife act upon hearing this kind of information? Would she be supportive? Fearful? Outraged that he let her go through with the ceremony and withheld this critical piece of information?

"I'll ask again. What does it have to do with you?"

"Nothing, Erin. They want to question me. I assume it's fairly routine."

I shake my head. "I always sensed that there was something odd about you and that Amelia woman. All the secrecy. I asked Madison about her. She said there was a resemblance to me. Why did you keep that relationship from me? And tell me again why you two broke up. Tell me everything again. Think of it as... practice."

"I told you, we split up over children. She wanted to focus on her career, and I was ready to start a family. We decided to break off the engagement and go our separate ways. Our split was unfortunate. It took its toll on me. But it was cordial. I promise."

"How did she die?"

"I have no idea. I don't have the details. Tanner said the police came to the house, looking for me. They questioned him. He said I was in Europe. They contacted me. I agreed to meet them on arrival, with my attorney."

"You agreed, or they insisted?"

Stefan shrugs. "Both," he says.

"What kind of career?" I ask.

"Huh?"

"What kind of career did she want to pursue that was so important to her she didn't want children?"

"Theater," he says. "She moved to New York City to become an actress. Now, is that all, Counselor?"

Stefan's smiling, but I can tell he's getting annoyed by my prodding.

But who wouldn't prod in my position?

My new husband's a person of interest.

In a murder.

The murder of his last fiancé.

His last fiancé who looked like me.

Inside, I'm freaking out, but I can't let him know.

So, I flash him a smirk, mirroring his playful tone,

keeping it light. "That is not all, Mr. Zeigler. Tell me about the last time you saw her."

He lets out a sigh.

"Seriously," I tell him. "You need to get your story straight for the cops. They might not take 'no comment' for an answer. Let's go through it. I'm a cakewalk compared to what they're going to do to you when we land."

"Fine. The last time I saw Amelia, she was heading back to the city. She packed up her car. She didn't have much to begin with, so she took what she came with and the clothes and jewelry I bought her. She told me she wanted a clean break and asked me not to contact her again. And then she drove away. That's the last I saw of her. I swear."

I drum my fingers on the armrest. It's not a great answer, and we both know it. "Can you prove that?"

Stefan tilts his head to one side. "I don't know. It was a year and a half ago. Any camera footage will be long gone. Maybe they can track her cell, if she used an app for the drive back to the city."

"And you never tried to reach her again? Or looked her up on social media?"

"I never tried to reach her. But come to think of it, I did see some photos pop up on my social media feed in the weeks after she left. Her accounts were still active, and then I deleted her. That's a good point, actually. I'll mention that to the authorities."

This is strange, because Stefan doesn't have much, or any, social media, aside from his professional LinkedIn profile. Did he close his accounts after Amelia left?

But I don't ask him about it. I'm starting to think playing dumb is my best option. Like my mother said, rich people have secrets. Ones you're better off not knowing. For now, I place my hand on his thigh and play the dutiful wife. He puts an arm around me, pulls me toward him, and kisses the top of my head.

"What's that for?" I ask.

"It was a good point, about the social media feed. I wouldn't have remembered that if you hadn't prodded me. You'd make a good defense attorney."

"We'll get through this, Stefan. Don't worry," I tell him.

Now if I can only get myself to believe it.

"Erin?" I call out from the front door, hoping that Tanner got my text, because he didn't answer me.

"It's open," Erin calls out. "I'm on the sofa."

I enter, and she's curled up in the fetal position, obviously in pain.

Rushing up to her, seeing the look on her face, I have a sinking feeling in my stomach. One borne of experience. "What is it? What's wrong?"

"I'm bleeding," she says. "And cramping, worse than a horrible period. This is bad, right?"

I let out a long sigh. "I'm not going to lie. It's not great news, but let's not jump to conclusions. I'll drive you to the hospital."

"I'm sorry, I didn't know who else to call. I don't have any other woman friends out here."

"It's fine. I get it. Let's get you up. Can you walk?"

"Yeah," she says. "But I'm so scared, Madison." Her voice is about to break.

"It's okay, Erin. It's all going to be okay," I say. I doubt that, but I'm trying to keep her calm. "Where is Stefan? Have you tried to reach him?" I ask.

"He's... busy. I can't get hold of him. Let me use the bathroom first."

My stomach sinks when I see Tanner's phone sitting on the coffee table.

Where is he? And this means he didn't see my text.

I pace around, looking for him.

Erin comes out of the bathroom. "It's getting worse. Let's go."

Tanner comes through the back door. "Hey, babe," Tanner shouts out to me. "What are you doing here?"

Glaring at him, I dart my head to my left, toward Erin, hoping that she didn't hear him, although I'm pretty sure she did.

"Hello, Tanner. I'm Madison. From next door," I call out, widening my eyes.

Tanner spots Erin on the sofa. Then I explain the situation to him, about Erin and her medical emergency, and that she can't reach Stefan.

"Oh man, I'm so sorry, Erin. I'll keep trying to reach him. I can call down to the police station. It's an emergency. They'll probably let him leave."

"The police station?" I ask.

"Not now," Erin says.

"Right. Let's go. Tanner, help me support Erin and get her to the car."

Leaving the legal issues for another time, I focus on Erin. She's moaning as I drive. When we get there, it's not very busy and they take her right away. I stay in the waiting room, but let her know I won't leave and that I'm here if she needs me. She tells me her best friend Lucy is on her way, and I assure her I'll wait until she arrives.

And while I wait, the memories come flooding back.

BETWEEN ABBY AND OLIVER, I had a miscarriage. Like Erin, I was a few weeks past the typical danger zone, and it caught me totally by surprise. The moment I let my guard down and stopped worrying all the time, the moment I started to tell people, the moment I started to envision Abby as a big sister, the universe knocked me on my ass, like I'd jinxed myself.

The funny thing is, once it happened, other women, even my own mother, finally admitted to me that it had happened to them, too. It's not something women tend to talk about much, as if talking about it might will it into existence, or somehow curse the next woman.

But that's not necessarily a good thing. Because I wasn't prepared for any of it. The physical pain. The soul-crushing emotional rollercoaster, fueled by hormone shifts. The loss. The guilt, going over and over in your mind every last thing you ate or drank. The power walk you could have skipped the day before. It plunged me into a deep depression.

It was the first chink in the armor of our marriage, and the reason Jeremy insisted that I stop working when I got pregnant again with Oliver, as if working causes miscarriages, when in reality, there is rarely a direct cause. I looked up the stats, and about 20 percent of women miscarry in the early stages. But still, you blame yourself, even with those odds.

And it keeps slamming you in the face, even when you've moved on. Because people still think you're pregnant.

It's not like you can just put a post on your social media feed and be done with it: I was pregnant. But now I'm not.

I actually said that once, in a business meeting. I was still working back then. And I had to postpone a meeting with a big client, due to a medical emergency, I told them. We were sitting around a conference table and they all kept badgering me.

What happened?

Are you okay?

We were worried about you.

It was bullshit. They were testing me, trying to see if I lied and went on a long ski weekend or a posh spa vacation. Finally, I blurted out those two sentences, and they all sat in stunned silence.

Then I added, "Now, can we get on with this meeting?"

Later, another woman joined me in the ladies' room.

"It happened to me, too," she said.

I nodded, but all I wanted to do was get the hell out of there. This wasn't the time or place for female bonding, especially with her. She always struck me as being a little off.

My hunch was confirmed when she said, "Did you want it? It's much worse if you wanted it."

What the fuck kind of question was that to ask a relative stranger?

But I was so flabbergasted, all I could say was, "Yes."

I SPEND the next hour or so reading a rom-com on my phone, trying to lighten my mood. Her friend Lucy arrives, and I fill her in. She heads in to check on Erin, and I ask her to keep me posted.

As I exit, it crosses my mind that Erin probably knows about my affair with Tanner. I suppose I need to get ahead of that, although since Jeremy knows too, it's not as big of a deal anymore. Agent Marino wants me to play along. Keep trying to get information from Tanner, but I want out.

It's not that easy, though. Now the local police are also involved, and they questioned me about Amelia Summers. It was almost as if I was a suspect, the way they were grilling me. I didn't tell them yet what Tanner told me, that he was sleeping with her. Maybe they'll think I killed her out of jealousy. It's all such a mess.

But it doesn't look good for Stefan. Or Tanner, for that matter. Both of them have motive. Tanner because of the inheritance and Stefan because of the cheating.

Which way will they go?

I'm not sure.

The police also admitted that it could have been a random crime, a robbery gone bad, after I pressed them about it. Her wallet was missing and she was found with no jewelry. I happen to know that Amelia liked her bling. So, it could be none of the above. Wrong place, wrong time.

That made me feel a little better. She flaunted her money and was killed for it. Rookie mistake. It happens occasionally, and she was the type. Not like Erin. Amelia was a real live gold digger. That makes me feel a little better about her fate.

One thing is for sure. I need to extract myself from the relationship. I told Tanner we can't see each other right now given the new developments, and he said he understood. Jeremy and I have settled for the time being on a marriage of convenience. My husband is staying in the guest suite, but we're hiding it from Abby and Oliver.

But I have a bad feeling about the situation next door, and I know it won't be easy to get rid of Tanner. Even if he's not a murderer, he's got secrets. So does his brother, and I know some of them. I could be in danger, and so could my family. So could Erin, and she went out on a limb for me.

I've been brushing up on my marksmanship, just in case. Another point of conflict in my marriage. Jeremy didn't want a gun in the house. But after a nearby home invasion, I insisted, and I finally won that battle. We keep it in a safe. That was the compromise; although the last few times I've gone over to Tanner's place, I dropped it in my purse.

Like this time.

Patting the hard metal under the soft, buttery leather, I smile.

Because if one of them comes after me or my family, I won't hesitate to use it.

THIRTY-THREE
ERIN

"Sweetie," Lucy says, patting my arm. "I'm here."

And it's then that I lose it.

My body convulses into sobs of sorrow, and I have to sit up in the ER bed so I don't choke on my own tears. Lucy rubs my back as I let it all out. The pent-up stress. The fear. The utter devastation at this loss.

And where is the father of my child through all of this?

Being questioned by the police.

After a few minutes, my tears slow to a trickle. I sniff up the remaining ones and try to get a grip. "I shouldn't have gone to Europe," I say.

"You can't blame yourself," Lucy says. "The OB told you it was fine. These things happen," she reminds me. "For no reason. All the time."

I know this is true, but I thought I was past the danger zone. It never occurred to me to wait on the marriage. That I'd marry Stefan because I was pregnant with our child—and then lose the baby. I wonder if he even knows yet. Madison said Tanner would try to get a hold of him. But right now, I'm more comforted by Lucy's presence. I'm not sure I even want to see Stefan.

"What do I do now?" I ask.

"Whatever you want, honey. Do nothing. Divorce the guy. It's all up to you. And I'm here for you no matter what."

"I need to call my mom."

"Whatever you want."

Then the reality hits me. After breaking my mother's heart by eloping, I have to tell my mom that her first grandchild is no more. It's almost too much for me, and I feel like curling up in a ball and ceasing to exist.

"I can't call her just yet," I say.

"One step at a time," Lucy says. "Is there anything I can do?"

"You can tell me everything you know about Amelia's murder," I say.

"Now? Are you... up for it?"

"Yes. Tell me everything. I have to know what I'm dealing with."

"The murder isn't federal. And I can't tell you how I know what I know. But it's not from Justin. It's from someone more local."

"That's fine."

"Amelia's body was found near Sagg Pond, in the Long Pond Greenbelt. But here's the thing. That wasn't her real name. Amelia Summers only started to exist about three years ago, as far as they can tell. But her description matched a missing persons case from around the same time, of a young woman from Wisconsin. I couldn't get the name. My source wouldn't disclose it. But it seems Amelia Summers wasn't who she claimed to be."

"Wow. Maybe she was some kind of scam artist?"

Then I remember Stefan saying she wanted to be an actress. I tell Lucy this. "Could it have been some kind of stage name?"

"Well, stage names, like pen names for authors, they aren't normally used on legal documents."

"Did she change her name? Legally?"

"I don't think so. From what I was told, she obtained fake ID, as Amelia Summers. But it would have had to be a good fake ID. And that's not easy to come by."

"What do you think it means?" I ask.

"Maybe she had some agenda. Maybe someone hired her to get involved with Stefan," Lucy says.

"To what end?" My mind flashes to Justin Peterson, Lucy's friend with benefits. I think about his efforts to get me to inform. "What if she was a CI? Or an agent, working undercover?"

"If she was, Justin's keeping that to himself. I told him about the murder. He didn't know about it. I know we're not exactly serious, but I know him pretty well. I think I could tell if he was lying. But here's another thing. Dimitri Petrov's estate is not too far from where they found the body."

"So, you think Petrov could have done it?" I ask.

Lucy shakes her head. "I have a hard time believing he would be that stupid. Maybe someone's trying to throw suspicion on him."

I swallow.

Someone like my husband?

"Did you find out anything more about Dimitri Petrov and his connection to Stefan?"

"Petrov filled a power vacuum after the collapse of the Soviet Union. Guys like him have done well under Putin.

He's in natural gas and seems to have some kind of business relationship with Stefan's father, who supplies natural gas to the EU countries."

"It's legitimate?"

Lucy shrugs. "I'm not even sure what that means anymore. There's nothing that would land him in an American prison, if that's what you mean."

"Stefan brought some paintings with him to his father's house. And he kept that from me."

"How do you know?"

"Stefan doesn't know this, but I have an app on my phone. It translates his German into English."

"Such a sleuth. You'd make a good CI."

"Stop! Can you tell Justin? Ask him about Petrov and the art connection?"

"What makes you think Petrov has something to do with Stefan's art business?"

"We ran into him at dinner one night, and he asked me what I did. I told him, and he gave me a card. Said he dabbles in art, whatever that means."

"I'm pretty sure Justin's told me everything he knows," Lucy says.

"Just ask him," I say.

"Yes, boss."

"Ask him what?" Stefan says, peeking his head around the curtain that divides my bed from the others.

My stomach sinks.

How long has he been standing there?

Thankfully, Lucy's an attorney, good at thinking on her feet.

"She wants me to ask my boyfriend to marry me," Lucy

says, rolling her eyes. "She can't accept that I'm hopelessly in love with myself and my freedom."

"Nice to see you again, Lucy," Stefan says. "Thank you for being here for her."

"Of course." Then she adds, "I'll always be here for Erin."

The two of them lock eyes.

"Good to know," Stefan says. "But I can take it from here."

"Of course," she says. "I'll give you two your privacy."

Lucy hugs me, and we say our goodbyes, leaving me alone with my husband, the murder suspect.

"Erin," Stefan says. He brushes the hair back from my face. "I'm so sorry you had to go through this alone."

I wonder if he's thinking what I'm thinking:

That we rushed into this marriage because of the baby.

That it was impulsive and rash.

That we don't know each other very well, if at all.

"This is very common," he says. "And we'll try again. As soon as you're ready. Don't worry, darling. It'll all be okay."

Nope.

He's not thinking what I'm thinking.

But then I'm not the one facing a potential murder charge. A woman with child makes for a more sympathetic defendant.

"How did it go with the police?" I ask.

"Good," he says. "I have a solid alibi. It was probably a robbery."

"Is that what they said?"

"Not in so many words. But yes, reading between the lines. Don't worry about that now," he says. "Just rest and heal. I love you, Erin. And I will spend the rest of my life trying to make you the happiest woman on the planet."

The rest of his life?

That seems to me right now like a long time.

A very, very long time.

THIRTY-FOUR
ERIN

My mother arrives today. I finally called and caught her up on everything. Well, not everything. Not that I fear my new husband might be a murderer. But I told her about losing the baby. She insisted that she come here to see me. I protested, mostly because I don't want to get her mixed up in all of this, and I don't want to put her in harm's way.

But now that it's looking more and more like a robbery gone bad, I feel a little better. Plus, Uncle Brody is picking her up from JFK and driving her here. I called Brody and told him about Amelia, and I asked him to explain it to my mother on the drive up, so she wouldn't be blindsided.

I didn't want to tell her on the phone. She's had some heart issues in the past. Brody said he'd handle it. And it'll be good for Stefan to see that I have family.

Family who will do anything to protect me.

It's been nearly a week since I lost the baby, and Stefan's been so great about everything, I'm starting to believe he had nothing to do with Amelia's death. It's what I would like to believe. I've already quit my job. It's not like I have a lot to fall back on, aside from Stefan and my marriage.

He said I should try to start up a business of my own, here in the Hamptons, and he offered his support. It seems he's not against my working, per se, and he wants to try again for a baby. I'm not ready for that, for so many reasons, but I've been skirting the issue.

Madison checked in on me yesterday, and some of what she said made me feel a little better, but some of it was a little concerning. I wasn't planning on saying anything about Tanner's "babe" comment. But she opened with it, after a compulsory check on my status.

"So, I bet you're wondering about me and Tanner," she said.

I feigned ignorance. "You and Tanner?"

"Don't play coy with me. I know what you heard, Erin. And I'm coming clean here. I figure I owe you that much."

"You don't owe me—"

Her hand shot up. "Just let me explain. Tanner and I had a fling. That's all it was. I was feeling empty and unfulfilled. It was impulsive. Retaliatory. Jeremy knows about it now. The kids don't. I'm not sure what's going to happen with my marriage, but I need to thank you for the wake-up call."

"The wake-up call?"

"My career. Getting back into designing. That's been a game changer for me. I have you to thank for that. Much more fulfilling than a fling."

"Oh, right." I'd totally forgotten that I'd given her the lead. "It worked out then? With the gallery owner?"

Madison shrugged. "Well, I got the job. I won't say it worked out until I have a satisfied client. But we're about halfway done, and so far, so good. I'm really enjoying being back in the city a few days a month."

I smirked. "This is so ironic."

"How so?"

"Now you have a job, and I don't. And I really miss the city."

Madison's eyes widened. "Oh? Was that your decision?"

"Nobody held a gun to my head."

Then I shifted the conversation to Amelia.

I asked her if she'd heard about the murder.

"Yes," she said. "Tanner told me. We're still... friends."

"What do you make of it? The police seem to think it might have been a robbery. What do you think?"

"It's possible. She was the flashy type. Always showing off her expensive jewelry. So, if anyone would have made themselves a target, it was Amelia."

I wasn't sure if I should disclose what I know, that Amelia wasn't her real name. But I decided to go for it. "Madison. I found out something about Amelia. If I tell you, will you promise not to tell anyone?"

Her eyes lit up and she leaned in.

Madison is the type that likes her salacious tidbits.

"Scout's honor," she said. "I know I can be a bit of a gossip. It sort of comes with the bored housewife role. But I know this is serious. A woman was murdered, and if it was one of these two, then we're both vulnerable."

"One of these two? You mean Tanner and Stefan? Why would Tanner be a suspect? Was he even living here then?"

Madison stiffened, and I could tell that slipped out accidentally. "He was living here, yes." She paused, like she was weighing out the pros and cons of telling me. "And he could have had a motive."

"What kind of motive?"

"You tell me yours first," she says.

"Okay. Amelia Summers was an alias. That wasn't her real name."

"What was her real name?"

"I don't know. My source wouldn't give that up."

She eyes me with an arched brow. "Your source? What are you, some kind of undercover agent?"

I shrugged. "If I was, I wouldn't tell you. Now it's your turn."

"Fair enough. Tanner said there's some kind of stepped-up clause in the family trust. Stefan gets more money for producing an heir. So, Tanner could have wanted to... get her out of the way."

My stomach sank, and it made me suspicious of Stefan and his eagerness to try again. "Well then, if that's your theory, I'm probably next on Tanner's hit list."

Madison shook her head. "No, the way I figure it, you're a lot safer now that they found her body. I mean, one dead woman can be explained. But two? Only an idiot wouldn't be able to see that. And Tanner's under a microscope with the house arrest. The feds are watching both of them. It's like flying after a big plane crash. Safest time. Everyone's on their best behavior. Don't worry."

She made a fair point.

Then I told her a little about the father, the controlling prenup, the natural gas business, the comment about Dachau, and what Stefan said about his family history. I didn't tell her about the secret painting.

"Fucking Nazis, all of them," Madison said. "They all say they weren't, but what are they going to say?" Then she added, "It's kind of a sore spot, given my family background."

She didn't elaborate, but I could read between the lines.

"Have you heard of a guy named Dimitri Petrov?" I asked.

She told me she had, and she recounted what I already knew. Petrov is a Russian oligarch with a yacht and a veil of secrecy around him and his business dealings. I told her that Stefan's done some business with him. And I pointed out that Amelia's body was found not too far from his estate.

"Do you think he's dangerous?" I asked.

"Petrov?"

I nodded.

"Not unless you cross him. Give him a wide berth and you'll be fine."

Just then, we noticed Tanner.

My stomach sank, fearing that he might have heard the tail end of our conversation, about Petrov. But so what? It's not a state secret that I harbor some concerns about the man. And then I remembered that Stefan thought Tanner might have tipped off Petrov as to where we were going that evening.

But why?

To what end?

Tanner and Madison greeted each other, and then she excused herself, leaving me in the awkward position of having to make small talk with my brother-in-law. He asked me how I was feeling, and I said I was fine. Then he walked past me and into the kitchen.

I could hear him making a cappuccino. I didn't scurry off to my room or anything. I didn't want to give him that kind of power over me. Rather, I picked up my book and started reading.

After Tanner got his coffee, he passed through the living area.

Before making his exit, he turned to me and said, "Erin. Don't go looking for trouble, and you'll be just fine here."

And with that, he exited the French doors and sauntered back to his cabana.

As I'm going over everything I know, trying to make some sense of a bunch of random facts, I realize Tanner could be at the center of all of it.

It's obvious that Tanner has a chip on his shoulder. He's been trying to turn me against Stefan from the moment I stepped foot in the house.

Tanner and Petrov could have had some kind of deal, regarding the art forgery. And Amelia could have double-crossed them, or figured it out and went to Stefan. I wonder if I should voice my concerns to my husband, tell him about the warnings from Tanner.

But what if Tanner's telling the truth?

If only I knew who to trust.

I HEAR A CAR DRIVE UP, snapping me out of my reminiscence.

Mom and Brody have arrived.

Stefan's here in the house, somewhere. I'm in the living room and I haven't seen him for the last hour or so.

The car doors slam shut.

I can hear Mom already.

She's a loud talker, and so is Uncle Brody.

They are going on and on about the route Brody took, with my mother insisting that it would have been faster going a different way.

"What's the matter with you? I used the app," Brody says. "We're here, aren't we?"

"Those apps are a scam," Mom replies. "They program it for the advertisers."

"What advertisers? There's no advertisers," Brody says.

"That's what they want you to think," Mom shoots back. "Don't be such a stooge."

Their banter brings a smile to my face, for the first time in days. And I realize how radically different my family is from Stefan's.

It makes me understand my mother a little better, and why she always warned me off the big money types. Nobody feels uncomfortable at our family gatherings. Not like I felt in Germany, or like I sometimes do in my own home these days.

I greet them at the door.

"Sweetheart," Mom says. She gives me a kiss. Brody's hands are full with her luggage, so I escape the compulsory cheek pinch.

Stefan appears at my side.

"So," Mom says to him, her hands firmly on her hips. "Are you the murder suspect who married my only child without my presence?"

To my surprise, Stefan smiles, a real one that reaches the eyes. "I am indeed the murder suspect who married your only child, Mrs. Donovan. But the elopement was Erin's idea, and in these matters, I think it's best if groom acquiesces, wouldn't you agree? Please. Come in."

THIRTY-FIVE
ERIN

This has to be one of the strangest days of my life.

Stefan continues to charm my mother.

Brody and Tanner are chatting it up like a pair of freshman boys on pledge night.

And I'm pretty sure that it's all for show.

I barely got a chance to talk to the two of them alone, but Mom and Brody assured me that they came armed for battle, and they'd try their best to get something useful out of Stefan and Tanner. They've obviously gone the honey route, at least for now.

We're out by the pool, Mom and I in lounge chairs. Stefan, Brody, and Tanner seated around his large, round plexiglass table, its green-and-white-striped umbrella fanning out over their heads. Stefan is close to me, so close that his hand rests on my arm.

The weather is a bit warm for early fall. One of those days that harken back to the middle of summer. When the sun slips behind a white, fluffy cloud, there's a chill in the air, but right now, with the sun shining overhead, it's warm.

I take off my sweater, displacing Stefan's hand.

"So. When is this wedding celebration party that's supposed to placate me after missing my only child's wedding ceremony?" Mom says.

The party.

Right.

Stefan takes my hand again, looks over at me, and then turns to my mother. "It's up to Erin, Mary. I'm not sure my wife feels much like celebrating at the moment."

Mom tenses up, ever so slightly. It was a dig, of sorts. He's accusing her of not being sensitive to my feelings. But I wonder why she even asked him that question. She knows I'm not in the best frame of mind for a party. She's not clueless. I bet it was a test.

"Of course," she says. "I'm talking about later. Not now. It might be nice to have something to look forward to. But of course, it's up to Erin."

When he looks away, she winks at me, then presses her lips back into a pout and crosses her arms over her chest.

I'm thinking it was a test—and he passed.

"I didn't mean to offend you, Mary," Stefan says. "And it's a good idea to have something to look forward to." Turning to me, he adds, "What do you think, honey?"

I shrug. "We'll talk about it some other time."

"So, Tanner," Brody says. "What're your plans after you get sprung? I had a cousin who was in on a gambling charge, before they made it legal. Stupid trumped up charge. He had a hard time getting work after. Maybe I could help you find something with the family, over in Brooklyn."

"Thanks. It's a nice offer. But I'm leaving town once I get this thing off me for good. Going back to LA. I want to get back to acting. My agent thinks I can milk it. It's not like I murdered someone. I mean, art forgery is hardly a crime. And Americans love their comeback stories. Just look at Martha Stewart."

"Yeah. They say any publicity is good publicity. Hey. Wait. Was it all a stunt?" Brody bats Tanner on the arm. "Don't worry, I'll never tell."

Brody laughs, a hearty laugh that reverberates around the backyard.

Tanner's jaw stiffens. "Funny guy," Tanner says, but he's not smiling.

"So, when did you find out that you two were brothers?" my mother asks.

I gasp. "Mom!"

"What? That's not something I can ask?" She throws up her hands, feigning cluelessness.

"Two years ago," Tanner says. "And I thought, hey, I've always wanted to try theater. So, I'll go to New York, bond with my bro, and give it a try. And then Stefan took me under his wing. Got me into the art business. And then, well, we all know what happened from there."

"And you didn't know the art was fake?" Mom asks.

"No. I didn't," Tanner says.

"So why'd you take the deal?" Brody asks.

Tanner juts his chin toward Stefan. "Ask him."

Stefan clears his throat. "Our family didn't want the publicity of a trial, so we agreed that Tanner should settle, since we got him such a good offer. Six months here in the Hamptons." He motions to the scenery. "It's not exactly Alcatraz."

"The deal was bullshit," Tanner says. "I should have gone to trial."

"What's done is done," Stefan says.

"Easy for you to say," Tanner replies. "You're not the one whose reputation is tainted."

"I thought you said Americans love a comeback," Stefan shoots back.

They lock eyes, and Tanner's the first to turn away.

Now my curiosity is piqued. "Where'd you get the painting, anyway?" I ask.

"Some Russian woman I met at a bar in town. I'd never heard of the artist, but she said the guy was the next Kandinsky. I had no idea it was fake."

"Did she go down for it, too?" Brody asks.

Tanner shakes his head. "Nope. She vanished into thin air. Can we please change the subject?"

Mom sits up from her lounge chair and turns her body to face Stefan. "Speaking of people vanishing, what's going on with the murder investigation? Erin is my only child, young man. I have a good mind to ask her to move down to Florida with me until this all blows over."

Stefan's face turns serious, and there's a hint of melancholy settling in his eyes. "I understand, Mary. And if that's what both of you want, I'll support that decision. But I swear as God is my judge, I would never hurt a hair on her lovely blonde head."

He reaches over and twirls a lock of my hair through his fingers.

"Good to know," Mom says.

Stefan continues. "I've been looking my whole life to find what I have with Erin. And I'll do anything to protect her. This will all blow over. I promise."

"Amelia was a blonde, too," Brody says. "I saw a photo on the news. You like blondes, eh? My Peg was a brunette. May she rest in peace."

"Amelia wasn't a real blonde," Stefan says. "And that wasn't the only thing disingenuous about her. But my attorney says I need to keep my mouth shut about her." He taps his watch. "And I'm afraid I have to excuse myself. Business call."

"Yeah, I'll get out of your hair, too," Tanner says. "Leave you three alone. I'm sure you have a lot of catching up to do."

"We do, yes," Mom says. "We'll see you for dinner?"

"Sure," Tanner says.

As Tanner's walking away, Brody adds, "If you change your mind about my offer, let me know. We could use a guy like you."

Tanner flashes him a thumbs up.

I roll my eyes at Brody.

Brody gives me a cheeky shrug.

Mom smirks.

And now the fun begins.

Agent Marino is chomping at the bit.

I'm having a little fun with him, dragging out what I know.

We are at my house, since I no longer have to hide the fact that I'm a confidential informant from Jeremy, although the kids are at school and my husband is at work.

"How does this Erin person know about the alias?" he asks.

"I told you. I don't know. She said she has a source. That's all I know. The source wouldn't give her a name. Did you know about it?"

"And I told you. This isn't a two-way street," he says.

He didn't know.

"I need to know what we're dealing with. Erin might be in danger. I might be in danger."

"The murder's not federal, Madison. I told you."

"How was she murdered? You must know that much."

He rolls his eyes. "She was shot."

"With?" My brows rise.

"With a gun." Marino smirks.

I shake my head. "Obviously. That's all you've got, or that's all you're giving me?"

"Yep." He narrows his eyes at me, letting me know the conversation is over.

I sigh. "Okay. What do you know about Dimitri Petrov?"

"Why do you ask?"

"Because Stefan Zeigler does business with him. The body was found near his property. I was wondering if the families may have had some common interests. Erin told me they ran into him at a bar, and Petrov gave her his card. He said something about dabbling in art. Maybe there's a connection? Money laundering?"

Marino shrugs. "It's possible. Anything's possible."

"Do you think he could have—"

"Wait," Marino says. "The art connection. And the families. What exactly do you know?"

"Not much, except that Erin said Stefan's father stormed out when she mentioned wanting to visit Dachau. Then Stefan made some excuse for the father. Claimed his family had been traumatized by the occupation, after the war. It made me think about Nazis, because the Nazis looted a lot of art. So, I thought they were up to something."

Marino's brow furrows. "If it's what I'm thinking, it's not dangerous for you or Erin."

"What are you thinking? And don't tell me about any one-way street. This is my family. My life, Nick. I need to know what I'm dealing with."

"You've heard about all the looting by the Nazis. Obviously. A lot of the missing art was recovered, but a number of pieces are still missing."

"Yes, I know."

"Well, the Soviets looted a lot of art, too. During the occupation. And that doesn't get as much press. So, it's possible that Petrov is helping the Zeigler family recover German art that was looted by the Soviets."

I nod.

Marino continues. "It's a thriving business. Not only art that belonged to the Germans. Art that the Germans looted, that the Soviets looted from them. Who knows who it belongs to at this point."

"Is that legal?"

"Define legal. It's all about jurisdiction. At the very least, there would be tax implications, if the sales here in the States are under the radar."

"What about the murder? Do you think Amelia might have figured out what they were doing and tried to get a piece of it? She struck me as a bit of an opportunist. Maybe she tried to blackmail them."

"Interesting idea. It might give me more ammo to muscle in and find out what's happening with the homicide investigation, if I can convince them it ties in somehow to our federal one. But if you and Erin both keep your mouths shut and your noses out of their business, you should be fine."

"Well," I say. "That does put my mind at ease. And I'm afraid this is where we part company. Jeremy knows about the affair. I broke it off with Tanner. So, I'm officially resigning as your unofficial CI."

"Well, that makes me sad, Madison. I was enjoying our little meet-ups. Very much. But I'm afraid it's not that simple. I need to keep tabs on you, for your own safety, until the case is closed and Tanner moves out of state. He'll be a free man soon. And you'll be a free woman."

"What if I can get you a little closer to the situation?"

Marino cocks a brow. "Go on."

"What if Erin would be willing to talk to you?"

"You trust her?"

I shrug. "She's worried she'll be next. And I can't say I blame her. She's much more at risk than I am."

"You think you can get her to talk to me?"

"Maybe. I can feel her out. But you can't say anything about what she told me, about Amelia's fake identity. I promised I wouldn't say anything."

"Wait. Did you pinky promise? Because if you didn't, it doesn't count."

I roll my eyes. "Very funny."

"I'm not a middle school girl, Madison. I'll do what I need to do, if it comes to that. But I don't think it will. If Erin's as freaked out as you say she is, I'll be able to get it out of her. It's what I do, after all."

"Right. And I'm going to tell her we just met. That you approached me, recently. She doesn't need to know I've been at this awhile. What if I can't trust her?"

"That's fine."

"So, we have a deal then? I give you Erin, and my work is done?"

"We have a deal."

I don't tell Marino about the secret room or the valuable paintings that might be stored there. If I'm on a need-to-know basis, then so is he.

My little crush on Marino seems to have faded, though, and I'm relieved about that. Because I know now that the key to my happiness and fulfillment doesn't lie with a man.

It lies with me. Me, putting my kids front and center, cleaning up my act, and finding a way to live with what I've done.

THIRTY-SEVEN
ERIN

Agent Marino is a charmer, that's for sure, but I'm trying not to get sucked in. He works for the FBI, and he's not here to solve a murder, or to prevent one. He's a cog in a very complex federal wheel, trying to break something bigger than all of us. Someone like me is just collateral damage to a guy like him.

This is what Lucy has grilled into my head. She coached me, before I agreed to meet with him, at Madison's house on this chilly, rainy Wednesday afternoon. It's nearly October, and winter is coming in fits and starts.

Mom and Brody are gone, but before they left, we dissected what we knew and tried to put it all back together in a way that made the most sense.

I told them everything I knew. That Amelia Summers was a fake name. That Tanner has been giving me little warnings about Stefan since the day I moved in. That Stefan brought paintings with him to Germany and hid that fact from me. That Stefan's family may have been Nazis.

Both he and Mom aren't too worried about the father or what side the family was on.

"The war years were complicated," Brody said.

Then he circled back to the paintings.

"What do you mean, he hid them?" Brody asked.

"I mean, he didn't tell me about it."

"Then how did you find out about it?" he said.

I explained how I overheard Stefan on the plane, and then later, telling his father about it, both times in German.

He was impressed with my spy craft, but then he added, "But not telling you is different than hiding it from you. Why would he tell you? He doesn't tell you much about his business, from what you told me."

Uncle Brody made a fair point.

Then we got back to the bigger threat: Amelia and her murder.

I told them what Madison said, and it was clear she wasn't a fan.

Amelia was flashy.

Amelia was a gold digger.

Brody reminded me that Tanner is an actor; the surfer dude persona could be a smokescreen. He might be more dangerous than he seems. They both mentioned that the tension between Stefan and Tanner was palpable, likely stemming from the inheritance.

The problem is, the police can't get a precise time of death for Amelia's murder because so much time has passed. Both have alibis of sorts. Tanner was in the city at an acting audition. Stefan had a business lunch in Southampton the day she supposedly left town.

"Why don't you come to Florida with me in the meantime? Until they solve the case?" Mom offered. "I don't like any of this."

I told her no. For many reasons.

First, if I had to put my money on one of them, it would be Tanner. He's jealous of Stefan. He's already a felon. And he's leaving soon. Stefan's been good to me, if a little cryptic at times. And I think Madison's point is a good one, that they're not going to murder me with the feds and local police up their asses.

I pointed all this out to them.

Brody agreed with me. "She's got a point, Mary. Smart kid. And she should stay and get what's hers."

I try not to factor in the prenup, and that each year I'm married to him, I walk away with another sizable chunk of change in the event of a divorce. I quit my job, though. Gave up my rent-controlled apartment. Economically, I'm very vulnerable, even more so than when I first met him, so I'd be lying if I said it wasn't in the back of my mind.

Plus, Stefan loves me, I'm sure of that. He's not going to put a bullet in my head. And if he's a victim in this too? And I leave him and don't stand by as the dutiful wife? That will taint our marriage forever.

Still, I recount most of what's worrying me to Agent Marino.

Everything except the paintings Stefan brought to Germany and my concerns about his family's background, because it doesn't seem relevant.

I tell him about the fake identity. The inheritance issue. The warnings from Tanner. And then something strikes me, as Brody's warning echoes in my mind.

"Wait," I say. "Tanner's an actor. Amelia, or whatever

her real name is, came here to act. Could there be a connection?"

Marino's brow knits. "What are you getting at?"

"I'm not sure. It just seems like a bit of a coincidence, that's all."

"People flock to New York City to act. Lots of them. But still. I'll get the local police to look into it. You never know. Tell me about Dimitri Petrov," he says, changing the subject.

And here's where I need to be careful.

"I met him once. He was quite amiable. Gave me his card. Said he dabbles in art."

"What's Petrov's connection to Stefan and his family?"

I shrug. "They're both in natural gas. That's all Stefan told me."

He nods. "Anything about art? Or old master paintings?"

I'm pretty sure it's not a secret that Stefan does some procuring, and I tell him what Stefan told me. Part of his business is buying and selling old master works of art.

"As far as I know, his art business has nothing to do with Petrov. I know that Tanner wanted to get more into contemporary art, but Stefan wasn't interested. That was another source of tension between the two of them. That's the kind of art that got Tanner arrested. But what are you getting at?"

"The less you know, the better."

"What's that supposed to mean?"

"It means we have nothing solid on Petrov. But still, Amelia Summer's body was found near his estate. If you were my sister, I'd tell you the same thing. Don't follow up with him. Don't ask your husband a lot of questions about him. Just sit back and observe. Report back to me. Let the murder investigation lead where it leads.

"In the meantime, I'll look further into Tanner and the

Amelia connection. That goes for Tanner, too. Maybe even more with that guy. Don't tip your hand. Keep it close to the vest. Because the last place you want to be is between two brothers feuding over a multi-million-dollar family fortune."

"Maybe that's exactly what happened to Amelia Summers," I say.

"Maybe it is," Marino replies.

***

DURING THE INTERVIEW, Madison excused herself and went upstairs, at Marino's direction. Now that he's gone, she's pumping me for information.

"We should put our heads together," Madison says.

"What do you mean?"

"I mean, there's things I know that you don't. And I'm sure that goes the other way, too."

I'm not sure if I can trust Madison, but I need more information. So, I proceed with caution.

"Well, since it's your idea, you go first."

"So. You do have something?" she says.

"I do."

"Is it big?"

"Not really," I say.

"Mine is big."

"Well, I have what I have, Madison. I can't make something up. It's fine if you don't want to tell me."

But it's not fine.

I'm going to burst at the seams if she doesn't tell me.

She must feel the same way, because she blurts out, "Tanner was sleeping with Amelia. And he thinks Stefan knew about it."

My eyes nearly pop out of my head. I can't imagine Stefan taking that well, if he knew.

"How do you know?" I ask.

She presses her lips as she pauses. "Tanner told me."

"It could be bullshit. He's an actor," I point out. "Maybe he's trying to make Stefan look guilty, like he killed her out of jealousy."

Then I go on to tell her my theory, that somehow Amelia and Tanner knew each other, before she met Stefan.

"It's possible," Madison says. "It all goes back to the inheritance. Like I said, there's a stepped-up clause in the trust. If there's an heir, Stefan gets more money. Tanner's not in the will. He's been trying to find a way around that, talking to an estate attorney."

"What if he and Amelia were in it together? She seduces Stefan, and then divorces him and goes with Tanner when she gets the money?"

"What about the prenup?" Madison asks.

"It's pretty generous, except in the event of infidelity. At least mine is. For every year of marriage, it pays out more money in the event of a divorce."

Madison sighs. "Then why would she sleep with Tanner? I feel like we're missing something."

"Obviously." I shrug.

"And now it's your turn," Madison says.

"It's nothing compared to your jaw dropper."

"A deal's a deal," she says.

"Stefan brought some paintings with him to Germany," I tell her. "He gave them to his father and he didn't tell me about it. I told you, it's not much. But it's all I've got."

"Interesting. How do you know, if he didn't tell you?"

"Well," I say. "I understand more German than I let on. I didn't tell Marino because I didn't think it was relevant."

Madison eyes me, visibly impressed. "Wow. You're not some shrinking violet after all?"

"Me? No. Not at all. More like a Venus flytrap."

Madison smirks. "Good to know, since we gals are looking out for each other. Nice to know I've got a killer plant watching my back."

We hold each other's gaze for a few long moments.

Then she opens her mouth to talk, but she catches herself.

There's something more that she wants to tell me, but for some reason, she's holding back. I don't push her, though.

Instead, I tell her I need to get going, stand up and turn toward the door. A little reverse psychology. I know the type. She'll tell me sooner or later.

"Wait," she says, as I'm strolling toward the door.

Sooner, it is.

I turn to her. "What?"

"Tanner thinks Stefan might have set him up."

"Set him up? Why?"

She explains something to me about a provision in German law. Tanner can't be cut out of the inheritance, even if he's not in the will.

"Except in the case of a felony conviction," she adds. "Tanner thinks Stefan set him up, so he would be disinherited."

"I see. Why are you telling me this?"

"Because I think Tanner might be right. I know him pretty well. Stefan might not be the man you think he is. You helped me get that interior design account. I owe you one. And I can't shake the feeling that you might be in real danger. You know the brother? The one who died in a skiing accident?"

I nod.

"Tanner suspects that Stefan was behind his death."

My breath catches, because the look on Madison's face is a look I've seen before. A look of concern, like when she saw Oliver in pain from the jellyfish sting. Madison Bradford is genuinely worried about me—and that might be the most terrifying realization of all.

With nothing more to say, I excuse myself and continue out the door, too frazzled to mention what Tanner told me. He got played by a Russian woman, who later disappeared.

Stefan did business with Petrov.

Maybe it's true that Stefan set Tanner up to cut him out of the inheritance.

But that doesn't mean he killed Amelia, or his younger brother.

Does it?

THIRTY-EIGHT
ERIN

Stefan and I have settled into a routine of sorts. After I lost the baby, Max reached out and offered me my job back. I told him I wasn't interested in full time, but we came up with an agreement that's working perfectly for me. Part-time, mostly remote, but I go into the city once or twice a week. This means Stefan and I don't see each other every night; sometimes I stay in the corporate rental in the city. And that's fine with me.

He's been on edge lately. I can't tell if it's the murder case or if his true colors are starting to show, but it makes me nervous.

Just the other day, he said something to me about an event, as if he'd already told me about it, but I could swear he hadn't. It caught me off guard, because we'd been talking about something unrelated. Something about getting a new pool service because the one we have keeps canceling.

"We'll have to leave for the city by noon tomorrow," he said.

"Huh?" I replied.

His face hardened and he snapped at me. "What did I just say? Do you have a hearing problem?"

My jaw dropped. He might as well have slapped me in the face. "You can't speak to me that way," I shot back. "And I have no idea what you're talking about."

"The benefit. I told you about it last week, Erin!"

He rolled his eyes—and he didn't apologize.

This burned me up. I don't think he told me about the event, but even if he did and it somehow didn't register, that was no way to talk to your wife, and I let him know it.

I expected him to come to his senses and own his mistake. But he didn't. Instead, he stormed off, leaving me speechless and steaming. I thought about skipping the event, but I didn't want to add fuel to the fire.

So, I spent the entire next day getting ready, like a good wife.

For high society events like the one we were attending, you don't just throw on a dress and call it a day. First, there's the hair. Then the make-up, both of which you can't do yourself.

Then there's the beaded dress, so heavy and stiff, it's hard to even sit down. When I caught a glimpse of myself in the mirror, I hardly recognized my own reflection. My hair felt like a wig, and I had to wash it three times to get out all the hairspray and goop.

But when I slipped into the car, Stefan barely acknowledged my presence. He glanced in my direction, muttered something about being late, and went back to his cell phone. That stung. I spent the whole day getting ready, and he didn't even pay me a compliment.

Right now, I'm reflecting on something Uncle Brody told

me, back when I first met Stefan and found out I was pregnant.

"You can't tell anything about a guy in the first three months of dating," he cautioned. "It's not like we're intentionally trying to defraud. But when a guy's in that gaga phase, trying to win you over? That's not the real him."

So who is the real Stefan Ziegler?

Is he the charming family man who wants nothing more than to make all my dreams come true?

Is he secretly a stone-cold psychopath that has all of us fooled?

Or is he a regular guy, a flawed but decent human being, who makes mistakes and sometimes can't see them?

I suppose time will tell.

LUCY HAS some news for me, she said.

This is my day in the city, and I was planning to go back to the Hamptons, but she's persuaded me to stay and meet her for drinks after work. I want to fill my mind with happy thoughts, so we agreed to meet at the restaurant where I met Stefan and grab drinks and dinner at the bar.

It's not that crowded today, a Tuesday. She's dressed in her usual attire, a tight-fitting hot lawyer suit with a lower cut blouse, like she just stepped off the set of *Suits*.

"What's the big news?" I ask.

"Drinks first," she insists.

It's the same bartender from last time.

Since I'm feeling nostalgic, I order a champagne cocktail.

He remembers us, and he chats us up a little. I'm not in the mood, because I want to see what Lucy has to say, but I don't want to be rude. After a few minutes, a waitress waves him over to her station and he leaves us to our business.

"So," I say. "What's your big news?"

"I found out Amelia's real name. She was Shelly Lipton. From Milwaukee, Wisconsin. Seems as if she got a fake ID about three years ago. She's a scam artist from way back. Had some priors for identity theft. Worked as an escort for a while. A real charmer."

I swallow.

This is not at all what I expected.

"How do you think Stefan got mixed up with her?"

"She was in a theater group. Some kind of experimental improv. With Tanner. They knew each other. He may have put her up to it. Seducing Stefan. To what end, I have no idea."

"Wow. I wonder if Stefan figured it out. He'd be... furious."

Lucy shrugs. "If she really is a scam artist, and she's good at what she does, it's quite possible that she double-crossed Tanner. Took one look at that lush Hamptons lifestyle and decided to stay with Stefan for real. That could have infuriated Tanner."

"What do you think I should do?"

"Stay out of it. How much longer does Tanner have?"

"He's leaving in two weeks."

"Well then, I would say just wait it out. With the police investigating the two of them, they won't do anything to you. They'd have to be insane to try anything."

"That's what Madison said."

"Madison? The Real Housewives of Southampton Madison?

"She's not that bad," I say.

Lucy shakes her head. "She's everything that's wrong with the world."

"Well, we can agree to disagree."

"Oh, I almost forgot. I snagged some photos from Amelia's social media. This one might be the last she ever posted. The day before she went missing."

"Stefan said he saw some photos on her social media after she left."

"My people didn't find any. Sorry. This is all we've got."

Lucy pulls it up on her phone and I see a selfie of a woman with blonde hair who, truth be told, doesn't look that much like me. Her eyes are brown, not blue like mine. Her face is heart-shaped where mine is round. Very attractive, though.

She's wearing a vintage emerald necklace that looks expensive, and dangling earrings that appear to be laced with diamonds. Madison said she was flashy, and I guess she wasn't exaggerating.

But what really catches my eye is her left hand, resting on her chest—and the rock on her ring finger.

Because it's mine.

The ring Stefan gave me when he proposed.

I'm wearing a dead woman's ring.

THIRTY-NINE
MADISON

"I'm not surprised," I tell Erin.

She's just disclosed to me that Amelia, or the woman I knew as Amelia, was a scammer. A former escort, no less. Who met Tanner in an acting class.

This sends me into a tailspin, and the first thought that pops into my head is I need to get tested for STDs. Lord knows what that woman was exposed to.

How could he be such an idiot, to sleep with her?

To take such a risk?

But then it occurs to me.

He didn't know.

"Tell me everything you know about her," Erin says.

"We've been over this," I say. "I told you I didn't know her very well."

But I know more than I'm letting on.

"Tanner told you about the affair. Why?" she asks.

I think about this for a long moment, because it's a good question. If he killed Amelia, he would likely keep the affair to himself.

I sigh. "I could be wrong, but my gut feeling is that Tanner told me because he thinks Stefan killed Amelia out of jealousy, and that Stefan is out to get him. And I think Tanner's right."

"It could be a diversion," Erin says. "He could be saying that to throw suspicion on Stefan and away from himself. What if Amelia double-crossed him and wanted to marry Stefan for real? If she's a scammer, that would be the ultimate scam."

"True. Like I said, I could be wrong. But you asked for my opinion. And that's my opinion. Does Stefan have a gun?" I ask. "Because if Tanner does, I've never seen it."

Erin shrugs. "I've never asked him."

"He probably does. Lots of rich people do."

"Are you speaking from experience?" she asks.

I smirk at her. "Let's just say I sleep soundly."

Then Erin tells me she has a photo that her friend Lucy found. It was supposedly taken the day before Amelia left, or disappeared.

"She's wearing my ring," Erin says. "What do you make of that?"

I hesitate, weighing out how much I should disclose. "Okay, well, I knew it was the same ring. I recognized it when you first showed it to me. And my first thought was, 'I'm surprised she gave it back.' Because she seemed like the type who would take anything she could get her grubby little hands on and leave town. And now that we know more about her? That she was a scam artist? Well, you see what I'm getting at."

Erin's face seems to go a shade paler.

She puts her head in her hands, then looks back up at me.

"Even if Stefan didn't..." She blows out a breath. "Even if Stefan had nothing to do with her death, it's still creepy, wearing the same ring. But then, it's an heirloom. Stefan might have insisted that she give it back."

"Sure, Erin. Anything is possible. But watch your back. Be careful. Because Tanner's leaving in a week, and I know you're excited about that. But if my hunch is correct, when he leaves, you could be even more vulnerable."

With my words of warning hanging in the air, we wrap up our conversation and she goes on her way.

AND NOW I HAVE A DILEMMA.

I want to prod Tanner a little. See if I can find out more about how much he really knew about Amelia. It is possible that she double-crossed Tanner.

If she did, Tanner could be next.

And then what?

Where would it end?

I've made a lot of mistakes in the last year or so.

Everybody makes mistakes.

I'm trying to put this all behind me.

To make a fresh start.

And it's happening, in baby steps.

The gallery job wrapped up, and Tina Weston seemed pleased, although she's hard to read. She paid in full and didn't complain. But she's not the type to gush, and I'm not even sure I could ask her to be a reference.

I've made a new website, and she gave me permission to post some photos, so at least there's that. One of the housewives in my parent group asked me for a quote to redecorate her living room. Like I said, baby steps.

Truthfully, although I'm happy to be working again, interior design feels a little servile, and like I'm going backward in life. But for now, it's better than nothing.

The front door opens.

It's Jeremy, home early from work.

He's trying, more than I would have imagined.

"Hey," he says.

"Oh, hi," I reply.

We chat a bit about the kids. My business. It's not awkward anymore. At first it was, our interactions more like acquaintances, polite and formal. Now we're more like friends. But he's still staying in the guest suite. And we're still hiding that from Abby and Oliver.

"Want a cocktail?" he asks.

I shrug. "Sure," I say.

Jeremy fixes two martinis.

We sit on the sofa and he tells me about work and I catch him up on my potential new client. We share the relief we both feel because our kids are doing well at school so far this year. And it almost feels like a normal life.

Almost.

Until I think about Amelia.

I can't stop thinking about what Madison said.

She seems hell-bent on making me think Tanner is inno-cent in all of this.

Does she still have feelings for him?

I saw her over at his guesthouse a few days ago.

Maybe she didn't know I was home.

Meanwhile, I'm trying to figure out if Stefan has a gun. I suppose I could just come out and ask him. He's got a safe, and I don't know the combination.

There's a lot of things like that up in the air, and we need to take care of them. For instance, I'm still not on his checking account, and he's not on mine. Not like he needs my money, but still. And I have no idea if he has life insur-ance. Shouldn't married couples talk about these things? It hasn't even been a month. Maybe I need to give it time.

He's a hard guy to talk to, and I sense it might be a cultural thing. Sometimes I feel like he wants a wife from the fifties. A well-oiled baby machine, not a true partner in life. He's fine with my doing whatever I want with my career right now, but he mentioned again that as soon as I get pregnant, he wants that to be my focus. And I haven't been able to tell him that I'm not ready for a baby.

After all, Amelia told him that.

And look what happened to her.

Today, Stefan's in the city, so I'm doing some investigating. Looking around to see if I can find a gun, or, alternatively, if I fail to find one, which would make me feel a little better about Madison's warning.

Checking his office first, I look behind paintings. Open his desk drawers, which he doesn't lock. Who am I kidding? If he has a gun, I'm not going to find it here. It's probably up in the safe, which is up in our bedroom.

But then again, if he used it in a murder, he wouldn't leave it in a safe. That's the first place the police would look if they got a warrant.

So, I go upstairs and rifle through the drawers and closets.

Nothing in the dresser drawers.

Or in the nightstand.

There are a few shoe boxes on the wood floor.

I open them and see... shoes.

But then I hear footsteps.

Is Stefan back?

Shoving the boxes back in the closet, I head downstairs to find Tanner hovering around the staircase.

"What are you doing here?" I bark, a little louder than I intended.

"Well, hello to you, too, sis." He smirks.

"You scared me. Are you sneaking up on me?"

His look is confident. Cheeky, like he has something on me. "Are you doing something to be snuck up on?"

"What? No. I'm just... cleaning out the closets. Making way for the rest of my stuff. Some of it is in storage," I lie.

"You're a terrible liar, Erin. And I told you. Don't go looking for trouble. You know there are cameras in the house," he says.

Did he see me?

"Well, of course I know that. Not in our bedroom." I throw this out in the hope that he can confirm this to be true.

"No, but in his office."

Tanner must have seen me go into his office.

I try to think of a good reason for my being in there.

"I was looking for the marriage license. I need to finish some paperwork for Social Security."

"Good one. Tell Stefan that if he asks you why you were looking through his drawers. Don't worry. It'll be our little secret."

Tanner's giving me the creeps.

This almost feels like a threat.

"I don't need to hide this from Stefan," I say. "I'll tell him myself. And I'll also tell him that you were hovering around here, spying on me."

He laughs. "I'm outta here in a week, Erin. And like I told you, don't go looking for trouble. Give him what he wants, and you'll be fine. If you can't do that, you need to get out."

I'd love to tell the smug bastard that I know. That I know about him and Amelia and how they met in acting class. And it occurs to me that I should tell Agent Marino about it. I'm starting to think that Tanner and Amelia deserved each other. Maybe she got what was coming to her. Maybe Tanner will, too.

"Go back to your cell, Tanner." My eyes dart to the ankle monitor.

Tanner lets out a chuckle. "Don't say I didn't warn you, sis."

I wait and watch him walk back to his quarters, and then I decide to abandon my mission and take a more direct approach about my concerns.

I COOKED A NICE MEAL. Baked halibut, roasted potatoes, and some steamed veggies. Stefan looked pleased when he came home to find me, apron around my waist, spatula in hand. I don't plan to make a habit of this, but it's fun once in a while.

We've been making small talk, discussing our day, when I finally get the courage to ask him what I want to know.

"Hon?" I say.

"Oh, I know that tone, Erin. What is it?"

"Can I be honest with you? Do you want to know what's on my mind?"

He shrugs. "I guess?"

"Lucy showed me a photo of Amelia."

Stefan rolls his eyes. "This again? She's nothing compared to—"

"No," I say, shaking my head. "It's not that. It's just, she was wearing my ring."

"Oh," he says. "That was my mother's ring, Erin. It was very special to me. A family heirloom."

"Well, I was surprised, that's all. Because you told me she left with the clothes and jewelry you gave her."

"Well, an heirloom is different. I wanted that back. But I

can see how that might make you feel. And if you don't feel comfortable wearing it, we'll go out and get you whatever ring you want, and save it for our daughter."

I swallow.

Our daughter?

I'm very pleased at his reaction, though. It makes me feel hopeful.

"Thank you for understanding," I say. "It's beautiful. I don't want another ring. But it means the world to me that you offered."

"Of course," he says. "But tell me something. Why does Lucy have a picture of Amelia?"

"She's still worried about me. She spends her day with criminals. That's just her nature, so don't take it personally."

"Anything else you want to get off your chest?"

I think about telling him I'm not ready to get pregnant again, but I can't do that right now. So, I tell him about the checking account. And I use that as an excuse, explaining to him I was looking for our bank info in his office, trying to get ahead of any sabotage Tanner's planning to unleash on me. I can't wait for that man-child to leave.

"Sorry. Yes, let's do that this week. With all that's been happening, I haven't been as on top of it as I should be."

We share an intimate kiss and prepare to enjoy a romantic evening alone—until Tanner comes in the back door and spoils it.

"Look at you two lovebirds," he says, with a smirk on his face. "Don't worry. I'm just getting some ice. I turned off my ice maker 'cause it was too noisy, and now I'm out of ice."

Stefan rolls his eyes.

I shake my head.

One more week, and Tanner will be out of our lives for good.

FORTY-ONE
ERIN

I've been married a month when I get a phone call that changes everything.

"There's been a break in the case," Lucy says.

My stomach sinks and my muscles seize up, as if I'm bracing for a punch to the solar plexus.

Is this the moment I learn that my husband will be dragged off in handcuffs?

Or that my brother-in-law is much more dangerous than I thought?

Have I been living with a murderer?

"Some guy in prison confessed to killing Amelia. Said it was a robbery gone bad. He tried to rob her at gunpoint but she fought back."

"He just confessed to all of this out of the blue? Sorry, but this seems a little too good to be true."

"Well, no," Lucy explains. "He's in for a double homicide. They traced some of her jewelry back to him. He fenced it at a pawnshop. And once they had that, he made a deal."

"How do you know all of this?" I ask.

I can picture Lucy rolling her eyes, but I couldn't stop the words from leaving my lips.

"You know I can't—"

"I know. You can't tell me. Does Stefan know yet?"

"Not sure. I suppose? Maybe ask him. He's your husband, after all." Lucy makes a good point.

But the murder case is a slumbering beast, and we dare not prod it. It's as if the very mention of it will evoke its wrath and send it thundering around our home.

Instead, we tiptoe around the issue, making small talk and pretending that our entire world isn't about to come crashing down around us, when it can, at any moment.

Could this nightmare really be over?

I take a deep breath and sink my shoulders, releasing the tension I've been holding in my neck and upper back, turning my head from side to side.

"I'll do that," I say, and we wrap up our call.

I'm going to make dinner plans for tonight. Somewhere nice. This calls for a celebration. And I'm going to call Marino and tell him I'm cutting ties with him. I may even come clean with Stefan about the feds approaching me. Start fresh. Build trust.

He didn't do it.

Why did I doubt him?

Speaking of trust, I've been hiding something else from Stefan. He's been eager to try again for a baby, but I'm not so keen on that idea right now, and not just because of the murder case. In fact, I started on the pill again. A little stronger one than last time, given what happened.

We're not ready, as a couple. An accident is one thing. We would have figured it out. But there's no reason to rush it. We've only been together for four months. I'd like to enjoy the honeymoon phase which, up until now, has been tainted by Amelia's murder.

It's not like I've lied to him. Stefan's never asked me about birth control. But I have a feeling if he found out, he'd be upset. So I hide the pills. If he asks me straight up, I'll level with him. But there's no need to rock the boat.

I do need to tell him how I feel, though.

If we hadn't gotten pregnant, would we even be married now?

Tonight, we will shine a light on the darkness and get everything out in the open.

Tonight, we will start fresh.

***

"WHEN ARE you going to change your name?" Stefan asks.

I was about to ask him if he heard the good news about the murder case, and this catches me by surprise. We haven't talked about my name change at all. I suppose we haven't talked about a lot of things a couple would talk about if they hadn't been forced into a shotgun wedding.

We've just gotten seated at a cozy table with a bay view at a trendy spot in Sag Harbor. Vessels of various shapes and sizes rest in their slips, rocking this way and that with the tides. The view of Shelter Island in the distance fades with the setting sun. And I realize it's like this a lot with Stefan. He has a way of steering the conversation in the direction he wants it to go. His style is subtle but effective.

I shrug. "I haven't given it much thought."

"Well, you are planning on it, right? I don't think you should have a different last name than your family."

This hits me harder than I would have thought. The idea of giving up my family. My name. Joining in with a family I hardly know. Keeping my name seems like a remnant from a bygone era; most women from my generation take their husbands' names. And it's not like I'm hell-bent on making a feminist statement. It's just that it makes me realize this has all moved very fast.

But I don't want to start the evening on a sour note, with all I have to disclose.

What's the big deal about changing my name?

"Of course," I say. "It's just with all we had going on, it wasn't a priority. But I'll start on it this week. But let's forget about business right now. I want to celebrate."

His eyes widen. "Wait. Are you telling me you're..."

Stefan pats his belly.

"Oh. No." I shake my head.

How would I be pregnant again this soon?

That doesn't even make sense.

"So, what are we celebrating?" he asks.

"Well, I was waiting for you to tell me. But maybe you don't know?"

Stefan's look is somewhat between puzzled and annoyed. "Know what?"

I swallow.

This isn't going the way I envisioned it.

"The case, honey. They've solved it. Someone confessed to Amelia's murder. It was a robbery gone bad."

"Why would I celebrate this?"

"Well, it means you're... I mean, we don't have to worry anymore," I stammer.

My husband narrows his eyes at me. "I wasn't worried. Were you?"

He holds my gaze until I look away.

I struggle to make sense of his reaction.

"No," I say.

Our meals arrive, but I'm not hungry. I pick at my food while Stefan methodically chips away at his. First the steak, then the broccoli, and finally, the potatoes.

It's that way every time we dine together. One food at a time. I wonder if it's a kind of neurosis, or if it's health-related. I read once that eating the protein first is better.

But I don't ask him. We've drifted apart. We're like strangers at a business lunch. If we can't talk about something as trivial as why we eat our food the way we do, how can we talk about something as important as when to start a family?

We sit in uncomfortable silence for a while.

I eat a few bites of my salmon, going for the protein with what little appetite I have, that dietary tip fresh in my mind.

After a bit, Stefan says, "Erin. Is there something you want to say to me?"

What do I have to lose?

I put down my fork and clasp my hands together. "Yes, there is. An FBI agent approached me. He was asking questions about you and Dimitri Petrov. And that got me... concerned, given what happened to Amelia. So yes, I was worried about the murder."

"How long ago was this?"

"A week or so," I lie.

"What did you tell him?"

"Nothing. What could I tell him? I don't know anything. I said something about natural gas. That's not a secret, is it?"

"No, it's not. What does this have to do with Amelia?" he asks.

I roll my eyes. "Try to put yourself in my position," I say. "What if the situation were reversed? And you found out my ex was murdered? An ex I didn't tell you about? And I was doing business with some Russian guy who was on the FBI's radar? And her body was found near his estate?"

"I would trust you."

"Easy for you to say. You're a man. You don't understand how vulnerable women are."

"That might be true," he offers.

But he's not getting it.

He can't get it.

He's never felt that rush of vulnerability.

Like when a strange man stares at you too long on an empty street. Or when a drunk guy tries to plant a kiss on you or cop a feel in a crowded bar. Or when a man grabs your arm, a little too forcefully, just enough to let you know that you're no match for him on a physical level.

But Stefan is dying to be a father, so I approach this from another angle.

"Let me put it another way. Suppose you have a daughter. And she marries a guy she hasn't known for very long. And then you find out that his last fiancé was murdered, and he was the last person to see her alive. How would you feel, as a father? What would you do?"

He blows out a breath and nods. "Okay. I see your point. I'd hide her away with a bodyguard until the guy was cleared, and maybe even longer than that." He smiles. "So where are you with this FBI guy?"

"I told him that since the murder case is wrapped up, I'm no longer interested in meeting with him. And if he has any more questions, he can talk to you or your attorney."

"Good girl," he says. Then he traces my cheek with his

finger. "I can't wait to get you home, Mrs. Ziegler, so we can celebrate for real. And make some little baby Zieglers that I can protect from all the bad guys out there."

There's no way I can tell him now that I'm not ready.

One step at a time. For now, I'll take the victory.

Maybe it's not too good to be true.

Maybe our marriage can finally get back on the right track.

So, I smile, and try to ignore the nagging feeling in my gut that the look in his eye is something other than passion for me.

How would I feel if Madison hadn't told me about the clause in the trust for producing an heir? How would I feel if my mother hadn't been filling me with doubt and distrust about wealthy men my entire life?

Then I picture the first time I saw him, in the crowded midtown bar. The way our eyes locked on each other. The tingle I felt when he started walking in my direction. The pang of disappointment when I thought he'd been intercepted.

And for the first time in a long while, I smile and sink into it, letting my desire blossom and my optimism rise up out of the ashes of doubt and distrust.

"Let's skip dessert," I say.

With that, we abandon what's left of our meals, pay the tab, and head for home.

THE NEXT MORNING, Stefan leaves early for work, after a steamy, romantic ending to our evening. When I get downstairs, there's a present on the island countertop. It's wrapped in silver foil paper with white stripes, a white ribbon around tied around it and curled at the ends, but it looks clumsily put together.

I smile.

He must have wrapped it himself.

Then I pick it up.

No name.

No card.

That's odd.

I unwrap it, then unfurl the white tissue paper.

A glimmer of green flashes as the overhead light catches it, reflecting off the stunning emerald. It must be three carats or more.

My stomach lurches, and my pulse pounds in my ears.

It's a vintage-looking emerald necklace with a giant stone in the center.

The one Amelia was wearing in the photo.

What does this mean?

And who left it for me?

FORTY-TWO
ERIN

"Did you get my little gift?" Tanner says.

My wrist jerks, and I spill my coffee a little.

"You startled me."

"That was the idea," he says.

I roll my eyes.

The wrapping paper sits on the island, the necklace glimmering on its white surface. Stefan left early for the city. It's the last few days of Tanner's house arrest, and I probably should have gone with my husband. Being alone with Tanner is unsettling. He seems to enjoy sneaking up on me.

"Don't you want to know where I found it?" he asks.

"I'm telling Stefan about this," I say.

"Go ahead. Tell him. It was in his office. After you failed to find what you were looking for, I took another look. Found it taped to the underside of his desk."

"You're full of shit," I say.

He laughs. "I guess you'll find out."

"He probably got it back from the pawnshop," I offer. "The guy took a plea deal. There's not going to be a trial."

"Yeah. Sure. But if I were you, I wouldn't ask any questions. Just tape it back up there and keep your mouth shut."

You were sleeping with her, I want to say.

You met her in acting class.

But I don't.

"The case is closed, Tanner. Go back to L.A. and leave us alone."

"We're a lot alike, Erin. Much more so than you and Stefan. Maybe you should come with me."

"Over my dead body," I say.

He widens his stance, as if to box me in, although the space is too big for that. "You're not as big of a pushover as I thought you were," he says.

"No, I'm not."

Lifting up his palms and waving them around the room, he says, "You like all of this, don't you, Erin? You've been a working-class girl with her nose pressed up against the glass your whole life. Let me tell you something. I'd have been a lot better off if I'd never met Stefan Ziegler, and the same goes for you.

"My family is a lot like yours. You'd like my mom. Salt of the earth, just like yours. I don't want the money for me. I want it for her. To make her life easier. She's a widow, like your mother. And my biological father never gave her the time of day. You met him. You know what he's like. Heartless bastard, that's what he is. I know I can be an asshole, but I'm telling you. You don't know the real Stefan. And I don't care what that lifer said. Maybe he shot Amelia dead, but if he did, Stefan put him up to it. So be careful. And this is my last warning."

With that, he turns from me and heads back to his quarters, leaving me trembling, the glittering emerald necklace still sitting on the counter.

IT'S LATE when Stefan gets home. Almost nine o'clock, but I waited up for him. I plan to ask him about the necklace, but I need to see what kind of mood he's in first. The minute he gets in the door, I can see it's not a good time to broach the subject. He mumbles something about a long day, kicks off his shoes, and says he's going up to take a shower.

"Do you want to have a—"

Stefan waves me off before I can finish my sentence. I guess he's not in the mood for a cocktail. Tanner leaves in just a few days, so I hate to start a big feud between the two of them right before he leaves.

Why would Tanner be doing this?

Is there a chance that he's genuinely concerned about my safety?

Stefan has the means to hire someone to do his dirty work.

But Tanner stands to gain more if I leave. I'm the key to producing an heir, if he's not already disinherited.

Heading upstairs, I decide I'm going to tell my husband what happened.

But then Stefan's voice roars out from the bedroom.

Was ist das?

He sounds furious.

"What is this?" he yells out, in English this time.

Did I leave the necklace out?

I bolt up the remaining stairs, taking them two by two.

When I enter, Stefan's standing there with his palm out.

Holding my birth control pills.

"Did you go through my drawers?" I ask.

"No! They were sitting on your nightstand."

I most certainly did not leave them on the nightstand.

"Stefan, I... I'm sorry I've been trying to tell you—"

He grabs my wrist and clamps on, squeezing so hard, I cry out. Then he pulls me in by my forearm so I'm inches from his face. "You lied to me? Made me for a fool?"

His lips are pressed, and his nostrils flare like steam is about to blow through them, the anger so white hot, it sends a chill straight into my bones.

"You're hurting me!" I plead. "Let go of me!"

He releases his grip, turns from me, and hurls the pills across the room. Then he kicks over an occasional table. Glass shatters as the vase that sat atop it crashes to the floor.

"I... I didn't lie," I stammer. "We never talked about it."

"Do not mince words with me, Erin."

And I don't.

He's too angry.

I've never seen a man this angry.

Tanner appears at the doorway. "What the fuck is going on here?"

And then it occurs to me.

Tanner must have found the pills and left them out to put a rift between us.

"You. Stay. Out. Of. it." Stefan grits his teeth, like he's about to chomp off Tanner's head.

"And you keep your hands off her," Tanner shoots back.

Stefan grabs Tanner by the shirt.

Tanner pushes him off.

This is about to explode into a full on-brawl.

"Stop!" I cry out, stepping between them. "Both of you,

just stop it. Tanner, I know you put those pills there to cause a problem." Turning to Stefan, I say, "And you, you're falling for it."

They both shake it off, and we all take a collective breath.

This is a nightmare.

I'm right where I didn't want to be, literally in the middle of two brothers, feuding over a multi-million-dollar family fortune.

"I'm going to the city for a few days," I say.

By this time, Stefan's regained his composure. "It's late, Erin."

"Let her go, Stefan," Tanner says.

"And I told you to stay out of it."

"I'm going," I say.

"Of course," Stefan says. "I'll call for a car."

And with that, I pack a bag and leave the two of them to fight it out.

A fight to the death, maybe.

But it's not going to be mine.

"So, you're leaving tomorrow?" I say.

I'm feeling oddly sentimental about this. Tanner might not have been the answer to all my problems, but he did help me out of a dark time. He allowed me to reclaim my sexuality and made me feel desired again; after what Jeremy did, I needed that.

I meant what I said to Erin, too. She might be more at risk when he leaves. This sentiment is confirmed when Tanner tells me about an altercation a few days ago. Stefan found out Erin was on birth control and flipped out. Now she's staying in the city.

"Maybe she'll divorce him," I say.

He shrugs. "Maybe."

"That would be good for you, no? Less likely for a little heir to materialize and take more of the pie."

"I'm letting it go," he says. "I want my old life back."

I don't believe him for a minute.

"Tell me something," I say. "For old times' sake. Did you and Amelia have something going before she met Stefan?"

"Why do you care?" he asks.

"I have my reasons."

"What makes you think I did?"

"Because I happen to know you met her in an improv class. Before she met Stefan. And I'm not the only one who knows this. So, you may want to get ahead of it."

"The murder case is closed," he says.

"Yeah. Pretty convenient. A guy just confesses, out of the blue. Sometimes they take it back. It might be good to have a story in your back pocket, just in case."

Tanner rolls his eyes. "Yeah. Okay. We cooked up a plan. She'd marry him. Wait a few years. Then she'd divorce him and go with me. It was her idea."

"So what happened?"

"She changed her mind. Stefan can be charming, when he wants to be. And then there's this." He waves around the room.

"Pretty risky plan to begin with," I say.

"She played me, I'm sure."

"Do you think Stefan found out about what you were planning? Would she have told him?"

Tanner shrugs. "It would have been in her best interest for her to keep her mouth shut about how we met. But what do I know? The whole thing blindsided me."

"You told me Stefan found out about the affair, though."

"I think he did. But that doesn't mean he knew I was behind them meeting."

"What makes you think he knew about the affair?"

"They had a big fight one day. About her cheating. I figured the fight was about Amelia and me, but who knows with her. They didn't know I was in the house. I left for the city, for an audition, in the middle of their brawl. Amelia wasn't like Erin. She could give as good as she got. I wasn't worried about her.

"When I got back that night, Stefan told me they'd called off the engagement. He didn't confront me, but I could read between the lines. I didn't ask any questions. I had no idea she was dead. I figured she just cut her losses, after he broke it off. Stefan said she took all her jewelry and clothes and split. It was probably worth a lot. Pretty soon after, a Russian woman approached me with the fake art piece. When I got arrested, I figured Stefan set me up as payback."

"Did you know Amelia Summers was an alias when you first met?"

"Nope," he says.

"Do you think Stefan was behind her murder?"

Tanner shrugs. "Probably. But it'll never lead back to him. He's too smooth. Not like me. That's why I'm leaving. I don't have a death wish. And Erin should, too, if she knows what's good for her."

"Did you ever figure out what was in that secret closet of his?" I ask.

"Why do you ask?" Tanner says.

I tell him the working theory. That it's art that the Soviets looted from the Germans, after the war ended, and Petrov is helping Stefan get it back.

"If it is," I say, "it could land Stefan in some pretty hot water."

"It must be worth a fortune," Tanner points out.

"Sure, if you can unload it. It's not the kind of art a person can hang on their wall. It requires a certain type of buyer. The kind of person who will pay millions of dollars and then keep it to themselves, in a secret room. It's worth a fortune, and it's worth nothing at all."

"How do you know all of this?" Tanner asks.

"Oh, you know, we Hamptons housewives have an ear to the ground. But don't worry, Tanner. I want to move on. Just like you. Speaking of which, how does it feel to be a free man?"

He shrugs. "I miss the ankle monitor. I mean, I don't miss it, miss it. But I can tell something's missing. My ankle feels weird."

"That'll fade," I say.

"I'm sure it will."

Just like this bizarre chapter of my life.

Hopefully, Erin's smart enough to stay away for good. I'm happy Tanner's leaving and this little detour off my otherwise straight and narrow path is finally over.

We share an intimate kiss, one that's more like an ending than a beginning—for old times' sake. And I let myself remember the rush of pheromones I felt the first time he touched me. Tanner made me feel alive again, and for that, I'm grateful.

I wish him luck and go on my way.

WHEN I GET HOME, my front door is closed, but not locked.

That's strange. I thought I locked it, and nobody should be home yet.

Guardedly, I enter.

My breath catches when I see him standing there.

"What are you doing here?" I ask.

"We need to talk, Madison," he says. "Have a seat."

"Are you sure about this?" Lucy asks me. "You can stay with me as long as you like."

"Yes! Stop! It's been three days. He's apologized over and over. I need my computer. Stefan has a meeting today and Tanner left for L.A. this morning. If something feels off, I'll come right back."

An Uber pulls up to her doorman building, and Lucy holds out a small canister of pepper spray. "Take this."

I laugh. "Like that's going to stop a bullet? Besides, I have some at the house."

"Just take it." Lucy shoves the pepper spray in my palm as I slide into the back seat with my carry-on bag over my shoulder. "Text me when you get there," she says.

Then she glances at the bruise on my forearm.

The driver pulls away before I can reply.

The truth is, Tanner's not leaving for L.A. until tonight, but I didn't tell Lucy that. Partly because I don't want to worry her, and partly because I don't want her to know what I'm planning, because she'll only try to talk me out of it.

I believe Tanner, that Stefan's doing something illegal with those paintings of his. And I need something on Stefan I can use as leverage. Because the moment Stefan put his hands on me, I knew I could never go back to him, although I've been pretending that there's a chance.

But I'm not ending up with nothing, and according to the prenup, that's what I'll get if I initiate the divorce. I gave up my rent-controlled apartment, my full-time job, my independence, all for him. There has to be a way to get what's mine, and Tanner might be the only person who can help me, in the event Stefan refuses to be reasonable and alter the prenup.

Maybe if I promise to give Tanner a cut, he'll help me find something on Stefan. Something that would land him in prison, if he won't agree to be fair with me.

It's risky, but I'm not going gently into the night.

THE HOUSE IS STILL when I come through the door.

Too still.

Eerie still, like the eye of a hurricane.

Stefan's in the city, or so he said.

So why is the front door unlocked?

Something's off, I can sense it. The alarm is off. Maybe we're being burglarized. I didn't check the garage, though. Stefan might be here. If so, he'd likely be working at this time of the day. Maybe his meeting got changed to remote.

Entering Stefan's study, strange scents bombard me, knocking me off balance. Sulfur, like when a match is struck, but more like a whole book of them ignited. And a metallic smell, one that I can't quite place. Underneath it all, the more familiar stench of feces and urine. Bile rises in my throat as it hits me, what must have happened.

I look around, my sense of sight catching up with my sense of smell. Blood pools on the wood floor and seeps into the crevices, running along the lengths of the floorboards.

A door is partly open, to a room I didn't know existed.

A body lies crumpled at its entrance.

"Stefan!" I cry out.

Is it him?

Do I have this all wrong?

Did Tanner finally take his revenge, on the day he was planning to leave?

I rush over and gasp when I see his face:

Eyes open.

A cold, blank stare.

I touch him.

He's still warm.

Wiping the blood from my hand onto my jeans, I grab my phone to call for help. A banging sound stops me in my tracks. Coming from the garage, I think?

I need to hide.

There's no time to make a call.

The soles of my sneakers are laced with blood, so I tuck my phone in my back pocket and pull off my shoes. Carrying them in my hands, I step carefully around the oozing liquid and dash into the closet.

Catching my breath, I try to absorb the fact that I'm in much more danger than I ever could have imagined.

Because it's not Stefan lying dead outside this door.

It's Tanner.

Tanner has been shot dead.

That can only mean one thing:

My husband is a murderer.

And if he finds me in here, I'm next.

Someone enters the room. They are alone, so I still can't tell who it is. But it has to be Stefan. Unless it's one of Petrov's people, which could be even worse.

All I have to do is stay quiet and I'll be okay. Nobody knows I'm here—yet. But as soon as my car is spotted, they'll know. I have to get a text off to 911 or Marino or someone.

Madison.

I decide to text Madison.

She's always glued to her phone.

And right next door.

She can call for help.

I hear a huffing sound, and I'm sure it's Stefan. And the sound of plastic crinkling. He must be trying to wrap the body to dispose of it.

"Mist," he cries out, his German accent more pronounced than usual.

It's Stefan, that's for sure.

What is he thinking?

He'll never get away with this.

Is he losing it?

My hands are sweaty and I can barely move inside this small space. If I knock into anything, I'm a dead woman.

I manage to slide my phone out of my back pocket.

Slowly pressing my arm along my side, skimming the wall, I manage to get the screen in front of me.

Palming it with my other hand so no light peeks out the door, I type the words to Madison that will hopefully save my life.

> Stefan shot Tanner. I'm hiding in his office closet. Call 911.

And now I wait for help, as my mother's voice rings in my ears.

Be careful what you wish for.

She knew. My mom knew. She tried to warn me. I should have gone to Florida with her. And now look where I am. Stuck in a closet, waiting to be hunted down by my psychopath husband.

Footsteps tell me he's leaving the room.

The body's still here, I'm sure. There was no sound of him straining to move it.

So I wait, hoping Stefan doesn't go outside and see my car. Wondering if I should take a chance and try to grab something. Anything I could use for a weapon. Then I remember. I have the pepper spray Lucy gave me in my pocket.

And I'm not going down without a fight.

FORTY-FIVE
MADISON

It takes a moment or so for my limbs to catch up with my brain, which orders me to move, move, move as I take in Erin's cry for help. I've been keeping my Glock in a more convenient place. My purse, so I don't have to retrieve it from the safe. But for a long moment, I'm frozen to the sofa, unsure of how best to handle this.

Because the other day, after I said goodbye to Tanner, Stefan paid me a little visit. I don't even know how he got into my house. I nearly had a heart attack when I opened the door and saw him standing there.

The gun was in my purse, but if I went for it, he could have easily overpowered me.

"What do you want?" I asked.

"I want you to stay out of my business. Stay away from Erin. Stop putting crazy ideas in her head. I know it was you who put Marino on to her."

"I have no idea what you're talking about," I said.

"Have you told anyone our little secret?"

"No," I said. "That was the deal. Not even Jeremy. Nobody else knows."

"You better keep it that way. Do we understand each other? And stay the hell out of my marriage."

"Or what?" I said, instantly regretting it.

Because I realized then that my family was in a lot more danger than I'd imagined.

All I wanted was for Stefan to break it off with her. To leave that wanton whore homeless and penniless and expose her for what she was: an opportunistic home-wrecker.

And yes, when I told Stefan about Amelia and her infidelity and saw the look in his eyes, my stomach sank to the floor.

Because it wasn't a normal look, full of anger and pain, the look of a sane human being. It was ice cold and red hot at the same time. It sent a shiver through my bones. But I was angry. He said he'd take care of it, and when I saw his reaction, I had a feeling it wasn't going to be pretty. Up until they found her body, though, I wasn't sure.

About a week after I told Stefan about her cheating, Amelia vanished, and I didn't ask any questions. But later, I befriended Tanner. The curiosity got the better of me.

I wanted to know more about her. What made her tick.

What made Jeremy risk everything we had and sleep with her.

Tanner was hot, and he flirted with me.

The opportunity for a little payback dropped in my lap.

I got distracted. Stopped thinking about Amelia. Got my revenge on Jeremy in another man's arms. And now I find out that Tanner was sleeping with Amelia too? It makes me sick. Why did she come after Jeremy? What was her end game?

Tanner's the one who put Amelia up to the scam, which makes it even more puzzling that she went for my husband, when she had a fiancé and a lover.

Some women are like that, I guess. They enjoy the hunt. The challenge. She probably had a bad childhood.

What's Jeremy's excuse?

But back to Stefan.

He answered me, with a threat. "Let's just say if something unfortunate were to happen to your husband? And the affair came to light? That wouldn't look good for you. Especially if the shooter claimed you paid him to kill Amelia and your husband."

I knew then that it was true. He set Tanner up. He murdered Tanner. He murdered Amelia. He threatened to kill Jeremy, the father of my children. He won't hesitate to kill me, if he thinks I'm a threat to him. I'm the only one alive who knows he had a motive to kill Amelia.

Cold.

Calculating.

Inhuman.

That's what Stefan is.

He'll never let me be.

He needs to be stopped.

The timing of this is critical, so I only call for help right before I enter the house.

Why do they ask so many questions?

It's an emergency, not a job interview.

I tell the operator to stop talking.

"There's been a murder," I whisper.

Then I give her the address and end the call.

The front door is unlocked, so I step in and look around.

Slipping off my shoes, I make my way toward Stefan's

office, to the right of where I'm standing. But I hear him banging around in the garage, so I crouch behind the pony wall that separates the foyer from the living room, trying to slow my breath and stifle the panic welling up inside me.

Peeking around the corner, I catch a glimpse of Stefan heading back to his office. Slowly, I pad toward him in my stocking feet, my weapon at the ready.

This time, I'm prepared.

FORTY-SIX
ERIN

I hear the sound of tape whizzing as it's being pulled around its spool. He must be taping up the body in a plastic sheet.

"Put your hands up, Stefan. Nice and easy."

Madison?

Why did she come here by herself?

Is she crazy?

Why didn't she wait for the police?

"It's not what you think," Stefan says.

"Oh really? And what do you think I think?" Madison says.

"He was trying to rob me. I'm a homeowner. I'm allowed to defend myself and my property."

"Then why are you trying to wrap the body in plastic?" she asks. "You killed Tanner and you killed Amelia. Admit it," she says.

If he's going to confess, I'm getting it on record. Pulling up the recording app on my phone, I listen to my husband try to weasel out of it.

"Amelia deserved what she got. Tanner was trying to rob me."

"Sure he was. What's in the secret closet, Stefan? Nazi war booty? Is that your game? Did Tanner figure it out? Is that why you killed him? Or did you find out he was sleeping with Amelia? That she preferred him to you?"

"Amelia was a scammer and a whore. You know that as well as I do. She was playing me the whole time, and Tanner was in on it. They both betrayed me. They both deserve what they got."

"The police are on their way. Don't move, or I swear, I'll shoot you dead."

"Not if I shoot you first," he says.

A shot rings out.

Sounds of a struggle fill me with dread.

I hear a loud thud, like someone hit the floor.

This is all my fault, so I spring out the door to help Madison.

Stefan and Madison wrestle on the floor. There has to be two guns, based on what I heard them say, but I don't see either one.

It takes a minute for my body to catch up with what I'm seeing, and in that time, Stefan's flipped Madison over. He clamps his hands around her neck. He's squeezing. Hard. Her eyes bulge as she tries to kick at him. He's going to kill her if I don't do something. I see the gun now. I want to go for it, but I don't have time.

Instead, I pepper spray him in the face.

"*Agghhhh,*" he yells out, as his hands fly to his eyes, allowing Madison to roll out from under his grip. I only catch him in one eye, so he can still kind of see.

He's going for the gun, but I tackle him before he can reach it.

Stefan kicks and grabs at me, and he's strong, but he's hampered by his partial loss of sight. I can only hope that Madison got the gun, but it's a flurry of limbs and fingers and feet and hands. It's all moving so fast, I can't tell what's what. Stefan pins me to the floor.

Where is Madison?

Was she shot?

"Stop!" Madison shouts.

She's got the gun now, up against his head.

"Let her go, dirt bag, or I'll shoot you dead."

Stefan releases his grip on me.

I spring up and stand next to Madison.

"Get up, and put your hands above your head."

He complies with her directive.

Sirens wail in the background, getting closer and closer.

"Erin," he says. "I love you. I'm sorry I got so angry about the pills. Don't believe a word she says. Madison and that bastard brother of mine were trying to take everything from us. Tanner was robbing me blind. Madison's a liar. She killed Amelia, for sleeping with her husband. And she was in on the robbery with Tanner."

Shrieking sounds fill the air, rubber against pavement.

The sirens are deafening now.

How will they know who to shoot?

"Erin's not falling for your stupid lies!" Madison cries out. "It's over. What's in the crates, Stefan? Tell me, or I'll shoot you in the kneecaps. Is it the art you monsters stole from the civilized world?"

"We're the civilized ones." Stefan scoffs. "That was the whole point."

Madison grits her teeth.

Stefan looks amused, but he's deeply misread the situation.

Madison looks him in the eye. "You smug son-of-a-bitch."

She shoots him square in the chest.

And then she shoots him again.

FORTY-SEVEN
ERIN

Blood sprays the back wall.

Stefan sinks down to the floor.

I've never witnessed anything like this, and my body starts shaking uncontrollably.

"Madison!" I cry out. "What have you done?"

Even though he had it coming, the visual hits me, hard. Nothing you see in the movies can prepare you for the reality of seeing a human being shot to death, right in front of your face.

Madison turns to me, surprisingly calm. "Saved your life," she says.

My mind struggles to catch up with what happened. "The police are here. I mean, you didn't have to..."

She narrows her eyes at me. "Listen to me, Erin. I don't have time to explain what should be obvious to you. You would never have been safe, even if you divorced him, and neither would I. You know this. Deep inside, I know you do. Just follow my lead. It was self-defense. We gals need to stick together, right?"

I nod. "Put the gun down, Madison. Or they might shoot you."

She does as I say.

And it hits me.

Stefan won't end up in prison.

I don't have to bother getting dirt on him.

Because he's dead.

And I didn't even have to be the one to pull the trigger.

OFFICERS thunder through the front door like a herd of elephants.

Our hands fly up.

"We're in here," I cry out. "Don't shoot."

Footsteps pound in our direction.

As they enter the study, Madison speaks first. "He tried to kill us," she says. "And he killed his brother."

Her body begins to shake and she crumbles into herself.

If this is an act, it's a good one.

"Call agent Nick Marino with the FBI," she says. "We're both informants. The art is stolen," she says. "I think Tanner was trying to steal it, and Stefan caught him."

But the officers aren't interested in what she's saying. They secure the weapons and cuff us. Then they tend to the bodies, confirming what we both knew already.

Tanner and Stefan are dead.

I take a deep breath and try to slow my racing heart.

It was a fight to the death, just as I feared it would be.

And I'm just thankful it wasn't mine.

EVENTUALLY, we had a chance to tell our stories. The best we can figure is that Tanner decided, for his last act, to make off with some of Stefan's art. Marino came and vouched for us. The recording on my phone pretty much sealed the deal. Madison got lucky, because it cuts off just when I come out of the closet. On the recording, Stefan doesn't quite confess, but close. Madison tells him to put his hands up, or she'll shoot.

Not if I shoot you first, he says.

And that's the end of the recording.

After they took off the handcuffs, but before they questioned us, Madison did something that took me by surprise. She told Marino that she was making a claim on the stolen art. That if there was any reward money, she was entitled to it. Baller move, I have to say. She must be pretty confident that I'm going to stay quiet about what really happened.

And I will. I know that what she did was wrong, but it worked out pretty well for me. But now that Stefan's gone, I have to admit, I'm breathing a little easier.

After hours of relentless questioning, they finally released us. My house is a crime scene, so Madison offered me a spare bedroom. I took her up on it, but we didn't have a chance to talk. She wants to keep it all from her kids, until she and Jeremy figure out how to explain it to them.

I'm up early, and so is she.

"Coffee?" she says.

I nod.

"So," I say.

"You can say that again." Madison rolls her eyes.

"How are you doing?" I ask.

She shrugs. "It's weighing on me."

"Give yourself a break. He tried to strangle you. You

saved my life," I say. "If Stefan found me in that closet, he would have killed me. Of that much, I'm sure. Given the situation, it's understandable that you snapped."

She narrows her eyes at me. "I didn't snap. I defended myself. And you. If he lived, he could have gotten to you, even from prison. You'd have controlled his entire fortune. He'd never have let you get away with it."

I realized something, about five seconds after she shot him, although I didn't feel it was in my best interest to comment on it.

The prenup covers divorce, not death.

We were married.

Stefan is dead.

His entire fortune... is mine.

FORTY-EIGHT
ERIN

Lucy and I stroll around Bryant Park, one last time. It's late fall, perfectly crisp. Park goers mill about like they haven't a care in the world, and I wish I was one of them.

We aim for a black bistro table and chairs, heading diagonally across the stone walkway. A man with a small dog passes a woman with a German Shepard, too close to us for comfort. The small dog lunges toward the big one, yapping and baring its teeth, and we almost get tangled in the leashes.

I shrink back, spilling coffee on myself.

"Steady, there," Lucy says. "It's just a little dog."

We sit.

"I'm fine," I say.

Lucy eyes me. "You don't seem fine."

"Maybe a change of scenery will help," I say.

She shrugs. "Up to you. You can stay as long as you want, and you can always come back."

But I've made up my mind. "I need a change."

"You can afford a change?" Lucy asks.

I take a cautious sip of my coffee and nod. "His father

controls the trust, but the house belongs to Stefan, as well as some of his other assets. It won't be as much as I thought it would be, but it'll be more than enough. Until it all settles, I'll stay with my mother."

"It could have been worse," Lucy offers.

My breath catches. "You really think he could have..."

Lucy shakes her head. "I think you shouldn't go there. That's not what I meant."

"He ordered the hit on Amelia," I say.

"That's what the guy claims now."

I sigh. "How did I not see this?"

"Don't do this to yourself. It's over. You won."

My hand goes to my forehead. "I don't feel like a winner. I still can't sleep through the night."

Lucy puts a hand on my forearm. "It's only been a week or so. It'll get better. I promise," Lucy says.

I sit with this for a minute, as the magnitude of what happened starts to hit me. All of this insanity, and now I'm starting all over again. A single tear rolls down my cheek. "I'm gonna miss you, Lucy Chang."

Lucy wipes away my tear. "Right back at 'ya. Erin Donovan. And I'm not going anywhere. You've always got a home, back here with me."

EPILOGUE
ONE YEAR LATER

As it turned out, Stefan's entire fortune wasn't as much as he let on, but it's still more than I ever dreamed of having. His father had him on a tight leash with the trust, which is why he was so eager to produce an heir. He'd get a large payout if that happened and be able to carry on his lavish lifestyle.

He owned his house in the Hamptons, although there was a modest mortgage on it, his cars and boat, along with a nice chunk of change in his stock and checking accounts. With the life insurance, I'll be set for the foreseeable future.

But his business assets were tied up with the family. I could have gone after that, but I didn't. Before Edmond Zeigler could contact me, I had my attorney approach him and tell him I'd sign anything he wanted to release my interests in the family business. That was the last I heard of my former father-in-law.

Most of the paintings in Stefan's secret compartment were a mixed bag with provenances that were difficult, if not impossible, to trace. All except for two pieces, which seem to have been looted from a French museum by the Nazis.

So much happened during World War II. Art was looted, then looted again. Sold privately. Tucked away. And even in the best of circumstances, it's difficult to find the original owner of works that are hundreds of years old.

One was an outright forgery, but it's unclear if Stefan knew that or if he was duped. The remainder were authenticated. My best guess is that they came from Petrov, who had them smuggled out of Russia and sold them to Stefan and his father. But Petrov denies this, and there's no proof. He came out of this unscathed.

Madison got a reward for the two French paintings. A pretty sizable one. With the money, she started a non-profit to help families of Holocaust survivors. It was a brilliant idea, and so like Madison. Because she's made herself the executive director, and with her connections, she's been able to quadruple the money through donations, secure herself a prestigious job with a nice fat salary—and come out looking like a savior.

I suppose in a way she is a savior.

Mine.

She invited me to the launch party, but I declined. It's a part of my life I'd rather forget, and I've decided to give Madison a wide berth. Not everyone could shoot someone in cold blood and then get on with life as if nothing happened. I figure it's best to quit while I'm ahead. Last I heard, she was still living with her family in the Hamptons.

Not surprisingly, the guy who confessed to Stefan's murder had more to say after he found out that Stefan was dead. He made a deal to get moved to a more desirable facility, claiming that Stefan hired him to shoot Amelia. He had some evidence to prove this to be true, but why did he confess to begin with?

That part is a little fuzzy. Lucy's best guess is that Petrov or someone who works for him coerced the guy into confessing, or promised him perks in prison if he took one for the team. The logistics of the hit were arranged by one of Petrov's bodyguards who also went down in the investigation. Petrov denies any involvement, claiming that he wouldn't be stupid enough to hide a body near his own estate —a fair point. The bodyguard was extradited to Russia in a prisoner exchange. Very convenient.

There's still a part of me that hopes Stefan wouldn't have been able to kill me, even if he had found me in the closet. I think about how he tried to bargain with me in the end, and wonder if he ever had feelings for me at all.

I still have nightmares about that day, and I've been working with a therapist who specializes in PTSD to try and heal. The nightmares are less frequent now, but the trauma still lurks in my subconscious. I'm sure it's a combination of guilt and fear. The fear is subsiding, but I'm not sure the guilt will ever totally fade away.

We used my recording. Stefan's homicide was ruled justifiable, due to self-defense. I try to tell myself it was, in a roundabout way. In my private moments, my decision still haunts me. Stefan was a murderer, I tell myself. But then so is Madison, if you get right down to it.

Now, I'm trying to get on with my life.

I sold the Hamptons home and moved down to West Palm Beach, near where my mother lives. It's been an adjustment. Sometimes, I miss the city, but that's fading. I miss Lucy, though. She came down for a week when I first moved and helped me get settled, and we speak regularly. She and Justin are still doing their thing, and she seems content.

My new home is spectacular and serene, walking

distance to Summa Beach, which I can use virtually year-round, unlike in the Hamptons. It's a contemporary home, sleek and modern, with a kitchen that deserves a better cook.

But what really sold me is the lap pool, which I use daily, now that I don't have my smarmy brother-in-law lurking in the shadows. Perhaps I'll get bored and move back to Manhattan in the future, but I needed a change. And for now, this is perfect for me.

I've always loved art, so I'm toying with the idea of opening my own gallery. I realize that I don't want to answer to anyone right now, in my personal or professional life. I have an appointment with a real estate agent this week to look at some potential spaces and start crunching the numbers. That's enough for now. I finally have the time to explore, and I don't need to rush into anything.

Mom's here, like she often is.

It's November, but it's still warm enough to sit by the pool and relax. She's reading a romance novel. Her favorite genre.

Taking a break, I close my computer and join her.

As I plop down on the lounge chair next to her, I can't help but marvel at her transformation.

Who was she kidding?

She's loving this living in the lap of luxury lifestyle, even more than I am.

I prod her a bit, just for fun.

"So, have you changed your mind about being a rich guy's wife? You're looking pretty at home here, Mom."

Mom hits back, in perfect Mary Donovan style. "You're not a rich guy's wife, Erin. You're a rich guy's widow. And it doesn't get any better than that."

ACKNOWLEDGMENTS

My sincere thanks to the many people who helped me craft this novel and bring it to completion.

Thanks to my invaluable alpha readers Rick, Robin, Susan, Donna, and Anne, who offered excellent suggestions and encouragement. Thanks to Makayla and Gabe for their twenty-something viewpoints of the Manhattan dating scene. Thanks to beta readers Christina Yother and Angela Frank whose suggestions offered valuable ideas to make the manuscript better. Thanks to my fabulous editor at Books-GoSocial, and to the entire team for their expert advice in marketing and promotions.

Thanks to all of my advance copy readers on Booksprout and NetGalley who take the time to read my books and post their reviews. Thanks to fellow thriller authors Steph Nelson, R.G. Belsky, and Leslie Lutz for their beta reads, blurbs, support, encouragement and camaraderie. Please check out their fabulous thrillers.

Thanks to New York City, for all the great memories that I will forever cherish, and to all my gal pal friends who painted the town red with me. There's no place quite like it, and it will forever be my favorite second home.

Finally, thanks so much to my readers. You are why I keep writing, and I am so grateful for the time you take to read my books as well as rate and comment on them. I read all of my reviews and it helps me to improve, so please keep them coming. I really appreciate it. For updates, book reviews and special offers, please go to www.bonnietraymore.com and sign up for my quarterly newsletter.

ABOUT THE AUTHOR

Bonnie Traymore is an award-winning, Amazon bestselling author of domestic and psychological thrillers that expose the dark truths beneath seemingly perfect lives. Her novels explore jealousy, infidelity, murder, and the impact of psychological disorders.

On the following pages, please enjoy a sample of my upcoming release, *My Husband Is Going To Kill Me.* Monica has concerns about her husband's anger issues, fueled by a man she met online who may not be trustworthy.

ONE

MONICA

My husband is going to kill me.

Maybe not today, but someday.

I know it. I feel it in my bones. Or more like, I feel it in my gut, which is twisted with fear. I feel it in my hands, which are shaking so much, I don't think I can drive. I feel it in my heart, which is racing after drinking two cups of coffee on an empty stomach. I thought he was gone for the day.

Hiding away in a corner of the house after another one of his explosive outbursts, I try and keep my distance. So far, he's never hit me, but he's come close.

The balled fist, which he shakes just inches from my mouth. The face, flushed with cortisol and adrenaline and raw fury. The lips that disappear into a tight grimace. How can I ever kiss them again?

The implication is clear:

I can kill you with my bare hands, any time I want.

Don't tempt me.

Yes. It's true.

One of these days, my husband is going to kill me.

Unless I kill him first.

Andrew is gone for the day, and my fear has turned to anger as I pace around the kitchen, waiting for the kids to get ready for school. It's a nice kitchen, if a little dated, in a smaller four-bedroom house, on a lovely suburban street.

It's not big enough for our family, but we live in one of the most expensive zip codes in the country, so it still cost us a fortune. From the outside, it looks perfect, with its manicured flower beds and freshly cut lawn. We're not too far from the other homes, though, and I wonder if the neighbors heard us this morning. If they know that inside these walls, it's not so perfect.

There's a pattern after one of his blowups. First, I tremble with fear. Then I tremble with rage. Then I convince myself that I have to stay in for the kids. That relationships have ups and downs. That our life is pretty good. All couples argue, I tell myself. It's all in my head. He's never hit me. He'll never snap, unless he does.

Right now, I'm in phase two.

Anger.

I want to punish him.

But how?

Marriage is a strange arrangement, when you stop to think about it. Two people pledge to stay together forever. Till death do us part. I have a little chuckle about this.

Okay, if that's the way you want to play it.

Sure. Divorce is an option, if you want to give up half of your assets and cut your net worth in two. If you want to coparent and divide up precious holiday and summer vacation days with your kids. If you want to be one of those many divorcées on the dating sites, with one failed marriage under your belt.

At forty-one years of age, fourteen years in, how would I be viewed? Fourteen years is a respectable amount of time to be in a marriage. I'd probably present as a solid choice. Someone who could go the distance, and young enough to try again, if that's what I wanted. Maybe it's not what I want. Maybe the next guy would be even worse.

But death? Well, let's talk about that.

You get everything.

The house. The retirement. The life insurance. Plus, you get the sympathy. A widow at the tender age of forty-one, with two school-age kids to raise.

So, yeah, marriage is a strange arrangement, for sure.

Especially if your spouse is worth more to you dead than alive.

As I load the dishwasher and prepare to leave for the day, my anger melts into melancholy reflection. I think back on when Andrew and I first started dating. He was so attentive. So charming. Was it all an act, or did his feelings for me change? I've tried to get him to go to counseling. Deal with his anger issues. But he refuses. Tells me it's all in my head. That I'm never happy. So I've given up. Instead, I bury my hopes and dreams and fantasies inside.

Sometimes, they surface in my dreams. Like three nights ago, I woke with a shudder. A man was touching me in a way that felt firm and gentle at the same time, his face so close to mine we breathed in the same air. His passion, wound tight like a cobra, about to explode and ravage every inch of my quivering body.

But then Andrew's alarm went off and I was alone, curled up on my side of the bed, right up to the edge, as if even in my sleep I want to distance myself from him. I stayed like that, nestled in the afterglow of my dream, trying to keep the feeling alive. Trying to get back to my mystery man, but it was futile.

My husband used to make me feel like that. Maybe the dream was trying to tell me to work harder to get that feeling back. So, the next evening, I made an effort. Rather than coming home from work and washing off my makeup and throwing on my sweats, I donned a sexy sundress, touched up my eye makeup, and waited until he got home. He's a workaholic, and it was after eight-thirty when he came trudging through the door. The kids were in their rooms already. We could have had some quality couple time.

I tried to make small talk. Acted flirty. But he waved off my words, headed into the bathroom to take a shower, and then started reading in bed. I'm starting to feel that it's useless to keep trying. I'll focus on the kids. Keep my head down. Stay out of his way. In the meantime, I've found a little solace on the side. And who could blame me?

"Hey, Mom?" my daughter Trina says. She's thirteen, with a perpetual whine to her tone of voice. "Where's my jeans?" A mildly accusatory tone hangs in the air, but I don't push back. I'm too tired.

"I hung them in your closet, honey," I say. "Hurry. We need to get going."

We never talk about the fights. She must have heard us this morning. Instead, we bury it deep, letting the tension fester under the surface. It must be affecting Trina, and my son Noah. He's only eight, still in that phase where he adores his mom, but past the point where he'll show it in front of his friends. Last year, he would kiss me goodbye when I dropped him off at school. But this year, on the first day, he shrunk from me and bolted over toward his friends.

It's fine. I've never been a clingy parent. I see that in other mothers and it seems pathetic to me. Too needy. I like that they are growing up. Showing more independence. I'm looking forward to having adult children with whom I can discuss current affairs over wine and cheese. I'm not one of those women who looks at their baby photos and pines for the past. I'm enjoying the age my kids are now, even with the attitude I get from Trina. She's spunky, like I was at her age. A woman in this world needs a little spunk. I wonder if I'll ever get mine back.

If you'd told me when I was a young, single woman that I'd someday be cowering in a corner of my own home like a beaten-down dog, I'd have told you that you were insane. But I realize now that life is complicated, and we all make concessions as we mature. I just hope the ones I'm making don't get me killed.

TWO

MONICA

For the next two months, I'm working at a health care facility in Sunnyvale, which is about a thirty-minute drive from where we live in Menlo Park, California. My son is still in public school, and my daughter started at a private all-girls school in nearby Palo Alto.

We can't afford two prep school tuitions, and the elementary and middle schools here are great, so the plan is to do private high school, one at a time. I'm not crazy about the idea of gender-segregated schools, but it's a top school, and even people in Silicon Valley who aren't into girls-only education send their kids there. Plus, that's the only top prep school she got into, but don't tell anyone.

When I pull into the parking garage, I find a space pretty quickly in the physician's section. Before I get out of my car, I check my messages:

> Thinking of you.

Smiling, I plop my phone back in my handbag and head

to the hospital without responding. If there's one thing I know about men, it's that they thrive on a challenge.

Speaking of challenges, this is going to be a busy day, but that's life in health care these days. I'm a locum tenens radiologist, which is sort of like a substitute teacher, but for doctors. I fill in when doctors go on maternity leave or take a sabbatical, or whatever.

Before I stepped down, I was chair of a bustling radiology department at a teaching hospital, and I constantly felt like I was shortchanging someone. My kids, when I wasn't at home, and my patients and residents, when I wasn't at work. Andrew's a workaholic, and he rarely, if ever, pitches in with the kids or the home front, but now he complains that I'm not bringing in as much money anymore. Yet when I outranked him, he didn't seem to be too thrilled about that either, so it seems that I can't win with him.

Now, because of my stellar reputation as a neuroradiologist, I make a decent amount of money working an average of thirty hours a week, often working from home, but it comes in spurts. Like now, I'm working a forty-hour week for the next three months, covering a maternity leave. Then I'll take a break for a month or two and focus on my family. I'll never go back to that full-time rat race again, trying to split myself in two as the perfect mom and the perfect physician, never measuring up in either arena.

But although I make good money, it would not be enough to support my kids in Silicon Valley if we got divorced, and the bigger problem is, neither could Andrew. We bought our house in the wake of a downturn, when interest rates were low. Property values have increased, and so have interest rates. There's no way either of us could stay here on one salary.

And even with both of us working, our house is smaller than you would think because real estate is so expensive, and smaller than we need. When I work from home, because of all my computer equipment and the six monitors that I cram into that tiny spare room, it's hot as hell and totally uncomfortable to work, but Andrew commandeered the den as his home office, even though he rarely uses it.

He's got so much stuff, and he refuses to part with it. Our home is cluttered and claustrophobic. Every closet is filled to the brim, and I wonder if that contributes to our stress. We're on top of each other, all the time. Even when I'm home alone, I feel him all around me.

It's not that I want Andrew dead, per se. Just getting him out of my life would be enough for me; if we could afford it. If he would stop with his explosive outbursts. If I could have full custody of my kids. But we can't afford it, and he won't stop, and he would never agree to give up custody of the kids, so none of my options are ideal:

Stay with Andrew and hope that he'll never snap and pummel me to death.

Try to divorce him, and possibly send him over the edge.

Or somehow, get rid of him.

"Monica! You're here," the Chief of Radiology says, wearing a smile that does not reach the eyes. His name is Walt Baxter, and he's a total egomaniac. A little past his expiration date, he rides his reputation for all its worth, but I'm not impressed by what he did twenty years ago.

His powers of deduction these days are adequate at best, and the fact that he's chair is proof that it's still a man's world in radiology, one of the most male-dominated medical specialties in the profession. He's tired of it all, I can tell, and he can't handle the pace or the pressure. Me, I'm in my prime, in no small part because I've found a way to recharge my batteries, and I'm not going back to the way things were. Burnout is real in the medical profession these days.

"Hi, Walt. What've we got?"

"A busy day," he says. "They're all nipping at our heels."

Walt walks me to the radiology reading room, giving me the rundown on the priorities, then he rushes off. I pull up the queue on my screen and get started. Reading film after film, dictating my findings, I zone out and do my job. I'm very good at it, and I enjoy my work. The laser focus. The intensity of it all. I'm the first person to find out what's really going on inside the patient's body, and everyone is clamoring to get my results and take action. I work fast but I'm careful. I care about my job. I care about the outcomes. Work appreciates me, even if Andrew doesn't.

Soon, it's midday and I realize I have not eaten a proper meal since yesterday at lunch. I need to take better care of myself. When the kids were little and I was working full time, I was sick constantly, and I looked like death warmed over. Once this gig is over, I'm going to recharge in style. For now, I have to keep on going. Grabbing a Chinese chicken salad from the cafeteria, I pull out my phone and see another text.

Hey beautiful.

Smiling, I tuck it back into my purse and shove a forkful of salad into my mouth. I don't have much time. Looking up, I see a perky woman making a beeline for me.

"Hi," says a woman I don't recognize. "You're Monica Decker, right?"

"Do I know you?" I ask, covering my mouth, which is half-full of salad.

"I'm Shari," she says with a smile, "Shari Bukowski," like that's supposed to mean something to me.

"I'm sorry," I say, shaking my head. "I'm not—"

She offers me a dismissive wave of her hand. "Oh, it was so long ago, don't worry. But I never forget a face. We met during those crazy residency years. How is Andrew? How are *you*?" she says, sitting down, uninvited, placing her hand on mine.

Right. I think I remember her now? She was sort of mousy back then, but now she's a kind of quirky-cute and looks younger than she probably is. Younger than me, in fact. Not that I'm jealous, it's just an observation.

I'm reserved and selective about social interaction, and this is one of the reasons that I love my current work arrangement. It affords me the opportunity to remain detached, so I don't get sucked into people's work drama. I just do my job and leave. But once in a while, since most of the assignments I accept are in the Bay Area, I run into someone who knows me and I have to play along. This is one of those times.

So, we spend a good ten minutes reliving the glory days of my residency years. It was grueling, sure. But there was a sense of camaraderie in all the chaos. And that's when Andrew and I met and fell in love. Sneaking away for a quickie. Falling dead asleep when we got off our shifts. It hurts to fake it with Shari. To lie to her about how wonderful my life still is with Andrew, the superstar heart surgeon who holds people's lives in his hands on a regular basis.

She goes on to tell me about her life, although it's clear that I'm not interested. The woman still can't read a room. She's divorced. No kids. Doing the dating app thing.

"I'm so jealous," Shari says. "You've really got it all, Monica. It's slim pickings out there. Hold on to that husband of yours."

She winks.

Then she gets up and leaves.

And I have to wonder.

Does Shari know something I don't?

I never trust the perky ones. The ones who are too friendly. And if I'm remembering her correctly, she was a bit of a gossip. I need to keep a close eye on Shari.

A very close eye.

To find out more, please see my website for current retail availability at bonnietraymore.com,

www.ingramcontent.com/pod-product-compliance
Lightning Source LLC
Chambersburg PA
CBHW070530310726
48976CB00002BA/587